"I have been excee

Caleb said, closing the dista... reminded himself to think of Julie in an impersonal manner—to pretend she was his best friend's fiancée.

Julie's breath caught in her throat as he leaned forward slightly, towering over her. Making her aware of him in a way she had never before been aware of a man. She felt quintessentially feminine and emotionally vulnerable, but the odd thing was she didn't feel threatened. On the contrary, she felt…invigorated.

He slowly lowered his head and his lips touched hers with the faintest of pressure.

Fiancée, he thought. He was supposed to be treating Julie like his best friend's fiancée. Caleb struggled to force himself to end the kiss, but it became impossible when she trembled in his arms.

I'll get a new best friend, he thought foggily.

Dear Reader,

Celebrate the holidays with Silhouette Romance! We strive to deliver emotional, fast-paced stories that suit your every mood—each and every month. Why not give the gift of love this year by sending your best friends and family members one of our heartwarming books?

Sandra Paul's *The Makeover Takeover* is the latest page-turner in the popular HAVING THE BOSS'S BABY series. In Teresa Southwick's *If You Don't Know by Now,* the third in the DESTINY, TEXAS series, Maggie Benson is shocked when Jack Riley comes back into her life—and their child's!

I'm also excited to announce that this month marks the return of two cherished authors to Silhouette Romance. Gifted at weaving intensely dramatic stories, Laurey Bright once again thrills Romance readers with her VIRGIN BRIDES title, *Marrying Marcus*. Judith McWilliams's charming tale, *The Summer Proposal,* will delight her throngs of devoted fans and have us all yearning for more!

As a special treat, we have two fresh and original royalty-themed stories. In *The Marine & the Princess,* Cathie Linz pits a hardened military man against an impetuous princess. Nicole Burnham's *Going to the Castle* tells of a duty-bound prince who escapes his castle walls and ends up with a beautiful refugee-camp worker.

We promise to deliver more exciting new titles in the coming year. Make it your New Year's resolution to read them all!

Happy reading!

Mary-Theresa Hussey

Mary-Theresa Hussey
Senior Editor

Please address questions and book requests to:
Silhouette Reader Service
U.S.: 3010 Walden Ave., P.O. Box 1325, Buffalo, NY 14269
Canadian: P.O. Box 609, Fort Erie, Ont. L2A 5X3

The Summer Proposal

JUDITH McWILLIAMS

SILHOUETTE *Romance*®

Published by Silhouette Books

America's Publisher of Contemporary Romance

If you purchased this book without a cover you should be aware
that this book is stolen property. It was reported as "unsold and
destroyed" to the publisher, and neither the author nor the
publisher has received any payment for this "stripped book."

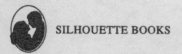

SILHOUETTE BOOKS

ISBN 0-373-19562-1

THE SUMMER PROPOSAL

Copyright © 2001 by Judith McWilliams

All rights reserved. Except for use in any review, the reproduction
or utilization of this work in whole or in part in any form by any
electronic, mechanical or other means, now known or hereafter
invented, including xerography, photocopying and recording, or in
any information storage or retrieval system, is forbidden without
the written permission of the editorial office, Silhouette Books,
300 East 42nd Street, New York, NY 10017 U.S.A.

All characters in this book have no existence outside the imagination of
the author and have no relation whatsoever to anyone bearing the same
name or names. They are not even distantly inspired by any individual
known or unknown to the author, and all incidents are pure invention.

This edition published by arrangement with Harlequin Books S.A.

® and TM are trademarks of Harlequin Books S.A., used under license.
Trademarks indicated with ® are registered in the United States Patent
and Trademark Office, the Canadian Trade Marks Office and in other
countries.

Visit Silhouette at www.eHarlequin.com

Printed in U.S.A.

Books by Judith McWilliams

Silhouette Romance

Gift of the Gods #479
The Summer Proposal #1562

Silhouette Desire

Reluctant Partners #441
A Perfect Season #545
That's My Baby #597
Anything's Possible! #911
The Man from Atlantis #954
Instant Husband #1001
Practice Husband #1062
Another Man's Baby #1095
The Boss, the Beauty and the Bargain #1122
The Sheik's Secret #1228

JUDITH McWILLIAMS

began to enjoy romances while in search of the proverbial "happily-ever-after." But she always found herself
rewriting the endings, and eventually the beginnings, of
the books she read. Then her husband finally suggested
that she write novels of her own, and she's been doing so
ever since. An ex-teacher with four children, Judith has
traveled the country extensively with her husband and
has been greatly influenced by those experiences. But
while not tending the garden or caring for family, Judith
does what she enjoys most—writing. She has also written under the name Charlotte Hines.

Jimmy,

It's me, Will. Remember that teacher I told ya about? The one my dad got to teach me a bunch a junk I don't wanna know. Julie, she ain't at all like what we thought. She can make cookies! Good ones full a chocolate chips and nuts. And she ain't always going on about drinking that disgusting cow juice. And she don't never yell, and when she smiles her eyes kinda sparkle.

I decided I's gonna keep her. All I gotta do is figure out how to get Dad to marry her so she'll have to stay. But I got a couple of great ideas to help Dad along. If'n you got any, write me back right away. I wanta get this settled before someone else grabs her.

Will

Chapter One

"Really, Mr. Tarrington! This is most irregular! You should not be here." The school secretary gave him a quelling look over the top of her bifocals that forty years of dealing with unruly grade schoolers had perfected. To her annoyance, he didn't even seem to notice.

"Yesterday was the day for parents to clear up irregularities," Miss Boulton persisted. "Today is the day that the teachers have to get all the end-of-year records completed and turned in. Miss Raffet is much too busy to see you."

"I won't take up much of her time," Caleb forced a reasonable tone despite the fact that he didn't feel the least bit reasonable. But venting the turbulent emotions churning through him on a secretary, no matter how aggravating she was being, wouldn't get him any closer to his goal. Which at the moment hinged on getting in to see Miss Raffet.

"Just see that you don't!" Miss Boulton's tone hinted at dire consequences.

She gestured toward the open office door behind him. "Miss Raffet's room is to the right. Fifth door down. Please stop back here on your way out and let me know that you're leaving the building. You wouldn't want to get locked in for the summer, now, would you?"

To her irritation, her attempt at humor didn't get any more of a response from him than her lecture. He merely nodded his head, gave her a perfunctory "thank you for your help" and left.

Miss Boulton watched him go, wondering what he wanted Julie for. Something personal? Something romantic? A flash of interest flared to life in her thin chest. Highly unlikely, she abandoned the idea almost immediately. Julie's little students might love her to distraction, but in the four years she'd been teaching at Whittier Elementary, Miss Boulton hadn't seen the slightest sign that a man might feel the same about her. Especially not one who looked like Caleb Tarrington.

She shook her head, effectively dislodging both Caleb Tarrington's unwelcome presence and Julie Raffet's romantic prospects from her busy mind as she reached for the internal phone.

Caleb paused outside the door the secretary had specified and took a deep, steadying breath, trying to organize his scattered thoughts. So much depended on him convincing the unknown Miss Raffet to help. If he couldn't...

An image of Will's pale face, his small features, rigid with fear he was desperately trying not to show, flashed through Caleb's mind, and a fierce surge of love filled him. His son! Even after twenty-four hours, Caleb still expected the words to be accompanied by trumpet fanfare.

If only… Abruptly he sliced off the unprofitable line of thought. The past was dead. Over. All the regrets in the world couldn't change it. All he could do was to try to shape the future differently. And the first step toward reshaping his son's future was to enlist the aid of Miss Raffet. Caleb just wished he knew a little more about her. All his old friend, John, had said was that she was the best first-grade teacher he'd ever seen in his career as a school principal. That if anyone could help him, Miss Raffet could. But the question John hadn't been able to answer was would she?

He'd soon find out.

Squaring his shoulders, Caleb marched through the door of Miss Raffet's classroom. He paused just inside the large, sunny room, his eyes instinctively going to the battered oak teacher's desk in front of the chalkboard. No one was seated there. His gaze quickly swept the room. The walls were stripped bare, and all the children's desks had been removed. The space looked abandoned.

He walked farther into the room, not sure what to do. Sit down at the desk and wait for Miss Raffet to return? Or go back to the office and ask the elderly dragon masquerading as a school secretary if she might have any idea where Miss Raffet could be?

Wait, he decided. Facing the disapproving Miss Boulton again definitely qualified as a last resort. Besides…

He turned at the sudden thump to his left. The noise

had come from behind a half-open door. A supply closet? he wondered. Could the elusive Miss Raffet be in it?

He watched as a woman slowly backed out of the closet. Appreciatively, Caleb eyed her trim hips, which were tightly encased in a pair of well-worn jeans. With obvious impatience, she shoved the door back and reached for something above her head.

Her action tightened the gray T-shirt covering her small breasts, outlining their perfection. Caleb swallowed, trying to ignore the unwelcome spark of sexual interest he felt.

Completely oblivious to his presence, she braced her slender legs and gave a hard jerk on whatever it was she was trying to get.

The thing she was yanking on suddenly came free causing her to lose her balance and land on her rear on the floor. A microsecond later, what appeared to be the entire contents of the shelf followed. Colored construction paper, yards of dusty white netting and some faded-looking plastic flowers bounced off her head and shoulders. Last to fall was a bag of gold glitter that broke as it hit her, sending gold dust everywhere.

It enveloped the woman, coating her light-brown hair and dusting her small, straight nose with golden freckles. Caleb blinked as the sun pouring in through the wall of windows behind her turned her petite figure into a radiant pillar of gold. For a heart-stopping second, long-forgotten Sunday-school images of angels welled out of Caleb's subconscious. Then she sneezed, and the explosive sound snapped him free of his memories.

"Drat!" she muttered in exasperation as she ineffectively brushed at the gold dust coating her.

"Are you all right?" The deep velvety sound of a man's voice poured over Julie, instantly smothering her annoyance. She instinctively turned toward him, squinting as she tried to focus through the glitter, which scattered at her abrupt movement.

Julie found herself staring at a large pair of black shoes. Not new, but immaculately clean and well shined. A part of her instinctively approved. Slowly, her gaze moved upward over long legs encased in suit trousers with a crease so crisp they must have just come from the dry cleaners. But this suit sure hadn't come from the local department store. She studied the way the jacket molded his broad shoulders. Obviously hand-tailored by an expert. Although she had the feeling he'd look every bit as good in a pair of jeans and a T-shirt. Or even better, dressed like an Italian courtier from the time of Lorenzo the Magnificent. All in velvets and silks and...

"Can you get up?" The worried note in the man's voice pulled her out of her daydream.

Julie winced, embarrassed at being caught in such an unprofessional position by such a gorgeous specimen of masculinity. She studied his leanly chiseled features with a purely feminine appreciation, wondering who he was. Certainly not someone she knew. Or anyone she'd ever met. She definitely wouldn't have forgotten a man who looked like the physical embodiment of every romantic fantasy she'd ever had. And a few she had yet to dream up.

"Did you hurt yourself?" he demanded, worried at her continued silence.

The concern in his bright blue eyes sent a shiver

of response through Julie. If none of the normal, garden-variety men she knew saw her as a sexy, desirable woman, then one who looked like this guy sure wouldn't, she reminded herself of a hard-learned lesson.

"I'm fine," she muttered, taking the helping hand he held out even though she was oddly reluctant to touch him. But not only would it be rude to pointedly ignore his gesture, but he wouldn't understand her hesitation. Any more than she understood it herself.

Even less did she understand her instantaneous reaction as his large hand closed around her much smaller one. Tiny pinpricks of sensation raced over her skin raising goose bumps as it traveled. Hastily, she pulled her hand back, breaking the disconcerting contact.

"You seem to be covered in this stuff." He gently brushed her hair, dislodging both a cloud of gold sparkles and her remaining composure.

Hoping he hadn't heard her quickly suppressed gasp, Julie hurriedly stepped back and made a production of dusting the glitter off herself as she struggled to recapture her teacher persona.

"May I help you?" Julie winced at the breathless sound of her voice. What was wrong with her? she wondered in confusion. She was acting as if she'd landed on her head not her rear.

"Not unless you happen to know where I can find Miss Raffet," he said. "This is her room, isn't it?"

"I'm Julie Raffet," she said, watching with a combination of annoyance and dismay as his eyes widened in shock at her announcement.

"You were expecting a little old lady wearing a

shapeless dress and orthopedic shoes?'' she asked dryly.

''Not really, but on the other hand, I was expecting someone who looked old enough to have graduated from college. And John did say that you'd been teaching for years.''

''John?'' Julie ignored her frustration at the proof that she hadn't even registered as an attractive woman with this man and, instead, grabbed the thread of his conversation that sounded the most promising.

''John Warchinski. He was principal here a few years back.''

''Yes, I remember him. Although I'm at a loss to understand why he should be discussing me with you, Mr....?'' Her voice rose, questioning.

''Tarrington. Caleb Tarrington.'' He stared at her for a long moment trying to decide where to start. He hated revealing the abject failure of his marriage. An older woman, such as that blasted John had led him to believe Miss Raffet was, might have understood how a normally levelheaded man could have gotten himself into such a mess. But this woman...

''Why don't you start at the beginning?'' Julie suggested with her normal practicality.

Caleb grimaced, knowing that the beginning had been an acute attack of plain old lust on his part, but he could hardly tell Julie Raffet that. She looked as if she'd never even heard of lust, let alone experienced it firsthand. She'd probably be disgusted at his admission. Or even worse, think he was in the habit of letting his sexual appetites overrule his common sense and refuse to have anything to do with him. And he needed her far too much to risk scaring her off.

He decided to gloss over the beginning and concentrate on the present.

"The beginning started with a youthful marriage that didn't—" Caleb made a gesture with his hand that conveyed a helpless sense of frustration "—work out."

Julie searched his face, looking for signs of pain at the memory of his failed marriage. She couldn't find any. Outwardly, at least, it appeared that he had recovered emotionally. But if that were true, then why was he finding it so hard to talk about it?

"I'm not doing this well," Caleb muttered, caught between embarrassment at being forced to reveal what he preferred to keep hidden, and the knowledge that if he wanted to enlist Julie Raffet's aid, he had to tell her enough to make her understand how desperate his need was.

"You're divorced?" The question escaped Julie's lips before she had a chance to consider the wisdom of asking. It wasn't that she wanted to know personally, she assured herself. She was simply trying to help him get to the point.

"Yes." The stark word sent through Julie a flood of contradictory emotions that she made no attempt to sort out.

"My ex-wife was an artist of considerable talent and, when she found out she was pregnant, she decided that marriage stifled her creativity. So she filed for divorce."

Julie arched her pale brown eyebrows in disbelief. "She thought marriage was too stifling, but motherhood wouldn't be?"

"Murna was into her Madonna phase at the time," he muttered obscurely.

Wrong, Murna was into her lunacy phase, Julie thought acidly.

"And you let her have custody of the baby?" Some of the anger Julie felt at the emotional mess two supposed adults must have created for their poor, defenseless child sharpened her voice.

"Murna said that the baby wasn't mine," he said starkly.

"And you believed her?"

"I had good reason to believe her! But even knowing about her affairs, if I had just stopped and thought... If I had insisted on a DNA test..." His voice was harsh with pain, regret and self-condemnation.

"I see." She felt an unexpected impulse to put her arms around him and comfort him. To try to ease the anguish darkening his eyes.

Don't get emotionally involved, Julie reminded herself of one of the cardinal rules of good teaching. One she broke regularly.

"But all that's history," Caleb said. "What's important is that yesterday morning without any warning my wife's lawyer dropped Will off at my office along with a document from Murna transferring custody to me."

Caleb's voice was flat, revealing none of the tremendous upsurge of love he'd felt when he'd seen his son for the first time. He hadn't needed the proof of paternity Murna's lawyer had offered. His relationship to Will was written on the boy's face for the whole world to see. No one who saw Will would ever mistake him for anything other than a Tarrington.

Caleb had wanted to throw his arms around his son and hug him. To try to explain why he hadn't been a part of his life before. But Will's rigid posture had discouraged any show of physical affection, and Caleb knew he couldn't try to justify his absence from his son's life by telling the child about his mother's lies. A six-year-old couldn't handle that kind of knowledge.

"To cut to the heart of the matter, Miss Raffet, the situation is this. I find I am suddenly responsible for a six-year-old son I know nothing about. Hell, I've never had more than a nodding acquaintance with any kid. Added to which, my housekeeper is an old maid who has never worked in a household with children."

"Single," Julie muttered. "We don't say old maid anymore."

Caleb didn't even hear her correction. He was too intent on making her understand the gravity of his situation.

"But the coup de grâce came this morning when I asked Will what grade he was in so that I could enroll him in school for next fall. And do you know what he said?"

Too agitated to stand still, Caleb began to pace back and forth in front of the blackboard.

"Be careful not to get chalk dust on your dark suit," Julie automatically warned.

"What?" Caleb glanced around as if surprised to find himself where he was. He gave her a rueful smile. "Then we'd be a matched set. Me in chalk dust and you in gold glitter."

A set. The curiously seductive word lingered momentarily in Julie's mind before she was able to banish it.

"My son said he didn't know what grade he was in because he'd never been to school."

"Kids say lots of things," Julie warned him. "Especially at six. Their distinction between fact and fantasy is not very firm."

"Well, he was dead-on with that particular fact! I called Murna to find out what was going on, and she said that she thought school stifled young minds. That she wanted Will to learn because he wanted to, not because he was forced to. So she simply registered him as a home-schooled student and left him to his own devices. She insisted that if I just leave him alone, eventually Will will learn everything he needs to know."

"An...interesting theory." Julie bit back her real opinion with an effort. Caleb Tarrington's ex-wife sounded like the most selfish, egocentric woman she had ever run across. She must have been monstrously beautiful for Caleb to have missed what had to have been warning signs of her self-centered personality. The thought unexpectedly depressed her.

"Why now?" The question suddenly occurred to Julie.

"What?" Caleb looked puzzled.

"Why suddenly give you custody of your son after all this time?"

"Murna's been commissioned to sculpt something or other in Venice, and she doesn't think Will would like it there."

Translated, it meant that dear Murna thought that a six-year-old would be too much trouble to drag around Europe, Julie thought angrily. So the woman off-loaded Will onto his father.

"Anyway," Caleb continued, "when I realized that Will was going to have to go to school not knowing what all the other kids knew, I called John, the only educator I know, and asked him for advice.''

"And John suggested me?" Julie said slowly, beginning to understand.

"Yes, he said you were the best first-grade teacher he's ever encountered.''

Julie tried not to be swayed by the compliment. But she was. John had never handed out praise with a liberal hand, and his comment was praise of the highest order.

"I want to hire you for the summer to teach Will what he needs to know so he can enter second grade next fall on a level with all the other kids his age,'' Caleb said. "It's going to be hard enough for him to adjust to living with a father he's never met, in a town he's never even heard of, without flunking the first grade through no fault of his own.''

"We don't flunk kids these days.'' Julie instinctively rejected the bleak picture he presented.

"So you plunk him down in the second grade where he can't do the work and let him constantly fail?'' Caleb demanded. "Is that supposed to be better?''

"No, of course not, and I sympathize with your problem, but I have plans for the summer.'' Julie tried to sound firm. She did have plans, she assuaged her conscience. She was going to landscape her yard. And she was enrolled in two graduate classes at the university. And she had a stack of reading material six feet high to get through. Her entire summer was overflowing with activities. Safe activities that wouldn't threaten the secure life she'd built for herself. Something she instinctively knew Caleb had the power to do.

"You can name your price," Caleb tempted her.

For one mad moment, a vision of her being enfolded in his arms filled her mind. Appalled, Julie shoved it aside. What was the matter with her? she wondered uneasily. Why did her attention keep drifting from what Caleb wanted to the man himself? She didn't have an answer and that bothered her almost as much as her unprecedented physical reaction to him. She wasn't used to her emotions going off on their own agenda. Usually they did exactly as they were told. Which was to stay firmly out of sight.

"It isn't a question of payment," she finally said. "It's a question of time. I really do have a lot planned this summer."

Caleb shoved his fingers through his dark hair in frustrated desperation.

"Please." He gritted the word out as if it were one he didn't use very often. "At least come and meet Will before you refuse to help. See what the situation is. Tell me what he needs."

Julie stared into the swirling depths of Caleb's blue eyes and was lost. His appeal, combined with the child's obvious need, made her retreat from a flat refusal.

"All right, I'll meet Will and assess his skill levels. But that's all I'm promising," she hurriedly added at his suddenly hopeful expression.

"Now?" Caleb asked eagerly, afraid to let her out of his sight for fear she'd change her mind.

Julie grinned at him. "You did meet Miss Boulton on the way in, didn't you? The only way I'd get past her without having turned in my end-of-year reports is on a stretcher."

"Tomorrow morning?" Caleb persisted. "Say, ten?"

"Okay," Julie agreed, and then swallowed uneasily as her stomach suddenly lurched, giving her the oddest feeling that she'd just stepped off a stair that wasn't there. She wasn't actually getting involved with Caleb Tarrington, she assured herself. Not really. All she had promised was to meet his son. She'd do that and then recommend someone else to tutor Will.

"Thanks." Caleb gave her a relieved grin that lit diamond sparkles in the depths of his blue eyes. Sparkles that momentarily seemed far more interesting than her carefully planned future.

Chapter Two

"Julie, any chance of you having lunch with me?"

Julie looked up, smiling at the unexpected sight of her older sister, Darcie, standing in the classroom doorway.

"I'd love to. Miss Boulton signed off on my materials list ten minutes ago, so I'm free. And starved. Let's get out of here before the woman finds something else for me to do."

"Why are you covered with glitter?" Darcie asked. "Are you starting a new trend?"

"Only for being caught in embarrassing situations," Julie said. "The stuff fell on me earlier while I had a visitor. I felt like a perfect fool."

"Nobody's perfect." Darcie grinned at her. "Although I will admit, you've improved enormously since you were a pesky little kid."

Julie grinned back. "I could say the same about you, but I'm much too polite. Although…"

She paused as it suddenly occurred to her that Darcie, with her active social life as well as her extensive contacts in the business world, might know Caleb Tarrington.

"What?" Darcie prompted as they left the classroom.

"What do you know about Caleb Tarrington?" Julie asked.

Darcie's green eyes widened slightly. "I know he's outside your league, Julie. Don't try to cut your teeth on him. You'll wind up breaking them."

"I cut my teeth, as you so inelegantly put it, years ago. And I have a perfectly valid reason for asking that has nothing whatsoever to do with what you are obviously thinking. Now, tell me what you know."

"Well, there's the obvious. That he looks like the answer to every woman's romantic fantasies."

The memory of Caleb's head tilted to one side, a lopsided smile softening his dark features, and his eyes gleaming with humor as he'd brushed the glitter from her hair popped into Julie's mind. She shivered slightly as she savored the image. No doubt about it. Caleb Tarrington was most definitely qualified to star in a romantic fantasy. Just not hers. She had better sense.

"True, but looks can be deceptive," Julie said. "Take me, for example. I may look like the proverbial girl-next-door, but beneath my prosaic exterior beats the heart of a dedicated career woman."

"Where are you parked, dedicated career woman?" Darcie shoved open the building's outside door, which led to the school's parking lot.

"I'm not. My car wouldn't start this morning, so I took the bus."

"No problem. I'll drive, and drop you off at home afterward."

Darcie unlocked the door to her sleek black luxury car.

"So what else do you know about Caleb Tarrington?" Julie asked once Darcie had pulled onto the road.

"I know that he inherited more money than he could ever spend. That he's an extremely successful architect. That he very quietly supports quite a few charities. But I don't know much about his personal life."

"Anything else?" Julie persisted.

Darcie grimaced. "I know blondes don't turn him on. At least, this blonde didn't."

Julie blinked. "You tried to..."

"Attract his interest is as good a euphemism as any. And, of course, I did. Any normal, red-blooded woman is going to have a go at Caleb Tarrington. It was at a Christmas party last year we both attended. I gave him my best sultry look."

"And?"

"And I could have been ninety years old for all the response I got."

"I find it hard to believe that someone as beautiful as you didn't get some reaction from him," Julie said slowly.

"Actually, I was rather surprised, too," Darcie agreed with her usual candor. "I guess it comes under the heading of you can't win them all.

"So tell me why you want to know about Caleb Tarrington," Darcie demanded.

"He came to see me today about his son," Julie said.

"His son!" Darcie yelped, and the car suddenly shot forward as her foot inadvertently depressed the gas pedal. "I didn't know he had a kid."

"He's six years old. Will has come to live with him, and Caleb wants to make sure the child has covered everything we teach in the first grade here," Julie said, reluctant to tell even her sister the personal details Caleb had given her about his marriage.

"And Caleb wants you to tutor the kid this summer?" Darcie immediately made the connection.

"Got it in one."

"Don't do it," Darcie said.

"Why not? Don't you think I'm a match for Caleb Tarrington?" Julie demanded, her pride stung.

"No," Darcie said succinctly. "Hell, I'm not a match for him, and I'm a hundred times more knowledgeable about men than you'll ever be."

"Not about six-year-old men," Julie said smugly. "And it's the six-year-old I'd be dealing with."

Darcie took her eyes off the road long enough to give Julie a rueful grin.

"I hate to be the one to break it to you, but most men are six-year-olds at heart. Besides, I won't be here to give you any sage advice if you do accidentally get in over your head."

"Where are you going?"

"The firm is sending me off the backwoods of Vermont to buy a patent."

"Well, you don't have to worry about me doing anything stupid. I fully intend to turn the job down. I was only curious about him."

"Just you remember that curiosity killed the cat!"

Julie chuckled. "Clichés yet. Where's your sense of originality?"

"Originality be damned. It's the truth, and don't you forget it."

Darcie's advice was probably right, Julie told herself. And it was definitely prudent. She'd enjoy her lunch and then go home, have a piece of chocolate and figure out how she was going to tactfully decline Caleb's plea.

Julie frowned slightly as she remembered the determined jut of Caleb's square chin. Maybe she'd have two pieces of chocolate.

Despite eating most of an eight-ounce box of truffles, by the following morning Julie still hadn't been able to think of a light, witty way to tell Caleb she wasn't going to help him.

Probably because she wasn't a light, witty person, she decided as her cab came to a tire-shrieking stop in front of the address Caleb had given her. At least, not when it came to kids who needed her help. But this time would be different. This time she would say no and make it stick.

"Hey, lady." The cabdriver broke into her thoughts. "This is the address you gave me."

"Sorry." Julie paid the man and climbed out, barely managing to get the door closed before the cab tore off down the street.

But Julie barely noticed. She was too busy studying Caleb's house as she slowly walked up the redbrick sidewalk that curved across the velvety, green lawn. Darcie had said that Caleb Tarrington was rich. Very rich. And Darcie had sounded very sure of her facts. Yet his house certainly wasn't ostentatious. The bottom story was built of a soft-gray limestone and the second story was white clapboard. The roof was a dark-gray slate punctuated by six attic dormers. Dark-green shutters outlined each of the oversize windows. The house looked like the comfortable, well-kept home of a professional, not the estate of a wealthy man.

Julie had no trouble imagining a child's bicycle lying on the grass or a baby stroller on the front steps. Maybe Darcie had her facts wrong for once, Julie thought, and then dismissed her speculation as irrelevant. Caleb Tarrington's financial status had nothing to do with her.

Julie nervously straightened her cream linen jacket, brushed the front of her blue silk shirt and then swallowed to ease the sudden dryness in her mouth before she rang the doorbell.

The door was jerked open before the melodious sound of the chimes had died away, and Julie found herself staring at the harassed features of a middle-aged woman.

"Yes?" the woman asked. Her eyes slipped to the bulging briefcase Julie held. "I never buy from door-to-door salesmen."

"A wise policy, I'm sure." Julie slipped into her best schoolteacher mode. "However, I am not here to sell you anything. I—"

"There you are." Caleb's voice came from behind the woman. It was threaded with some emotion that sounded suspiciously like desperation. He grabbed her arm as if he expected her to make a run for it, and pulled her into the house.

She'd been right, Julie thought distractedly. Caleb Tarrington did look every bit as good in casual clothes as he did in a suit. Maybe better. Definitely sexier. She studied his khaki pants and worn denim shirt with approval.

"You said ten o'clock and..." Julie used the excuse of checking the time to remove her arm from his grasp. For some reason, physical contact with Caleb Tarrington played havoc with her thought processes, and she needed to keep her wits about her.

"It's exactly ten now," she said.

Caleb grimaced. "Strange, I feel like it's been years since I got up this morning. This is my housekeeper, Miss Vincent. Miss Vincent, this is Miss Raffet. She's going to help Will get ready for school next fall."

Julie opened her mouth to remind Caleb that she had only agreed to see what Will needed to learn, not supply that knowledge herself, but before she could get out a word, a small boy got up off the sofa and walked toward her.

"My mom she says that school stifles creativity," he said. "I don't want my creativity stifled."

"I'd like to stifle more than his creativity!" Miss Vincent muttered darkly.

Julie blinked. For a child who'd only been here a day, Will seemed to have made quite an impression on the housekeeper.

Stepping farther into the house, Julie took a good look at Will. His thin frame held not even the promise of someday developing the muscles that shaped his father's body. Although his slightly oversize nose and his bright blue eyes had clearly been fished out of the same gene pool that had produced Caleb. But the expression of misery in the boy's eyes made Julie's heart contract with pity.

Poor little kid. How could his mother have just

given him to a man the child had never even met? Caleb's son deserved better. Any kid deserved better.

"Miss Raffet teaches first grade at the school you'll be going to in the fall." Caleb tossed the conversation gambit into the growing silence.

"And I promise our school tries to keep the stifling to an absolute minimum." Julie smiled at Will.

"My mom says that public-school teachers is incompetent!" Will eyed her challengingly. "My mom says they only teach there 'cause they can't do nothing else. My mom says I can learn everything I need to know at home all by myself!"

"Your precious mother— " the housekeeper began hotly, only to be quickly cut off by Caleb.

"We won't keep you anymore, Miss Vincent," he said firmly.

"Yes, sir," the woman muttered, and with a final, frustrated glare at Will, stomped out of the room.

Julie felt a sneaking sympathy for the housekeeper. Clearly, Will wasn't going to be easy to deal with.

Although, Julie studied Will's forlorn face, she didn't think he was being intentionally rude. Six-year-olds rarely understood the full impact of their words. Nor did they tend to think before they spoke. They just came right out with what they were thinking. Or with what they'd heard, and in Will's case, he seemed to have heard more than he should have.

"How about if we go out on the patio, Will?" Caleb used the bright tone adults reserve for kids when they haven't the vaguest idea how to talk to them.

"No," Will replied promptly.

"No, what?" Caleb stared at his son in surprise.

"No, thank you?" Will tried again.

"First lesson on surviving in the adult world, Will," Julie said, "is to learn about rhetorical questions."

"What's a re...ret...one of them?" Will asked curiously.

"It's a question that doesn't expect an answer. Like, don't you think it's time to go to bed? Or I'm sure you want to eat your spinach? Your father wasn't asking your consent for us to go to the patio. He was politely telling you to do it."

"And polite is getting to be in short supply around here this morning," Caleb said.

Julie looked at Caleb, her eyes lingering on his face. There was a line between his dark eyebrows, and she could clearly see the muscles knotted along his jawline. The brilliant glitter of his eyes seemed dimmed. He looked as if he'd had a bad night, followed by a worse morning. Maybe what Caleb needed was a few minutes away from his son. And her away from him. The second thought followed on the heels of the first. It would give her a chance to totally regain her teacher persona, which being around Caleb had ruffled.

"Will and I can..." she began.

"No," Caleb flatly rejected the idea before she could even formulate it. "Will is my son, and I want to find out firsthand what is going on."

"As you wish, Mr. Tarrington." Julie ignored the spurt of pleasure she felt as irrelevant.

"Caleb," he corrected her. "And if I might call you Julie?"

The sound of her name on his lips did odd things to her equilibrium. Somehow, shaped by his deep voice, her name took on an allure that she knew it didn't really have. It sounded mysterious and seductive, totally different from her normal practical self.

Mentally, Julie shook her head, trying to dislodge the fantasy. You are here to work, she reminded herself. Concentrate on the son. Him you can handle.

Julie's gaze dropped to Will, noting the belligerent thrust of his lower lip. He looked confused and unhappy. She wanted to assure him that everything would be all right, but she refused to lie to him. She had no idea if everything would be all right in his world. Nor had she any way of making it so. She shot a quick glance at Caleb, who was watching his son with a hungry longing, and felt fractionally better. If human effort could fix Will's world, then she didn't have the slightest doubt that Caleb would do it.

"What's you going to do?" Will demanded.

"Just read a little with you, ask you a few questions and play a few games," Julie said.

"I ain't ath…a…letical." Will stumbled over the word. "Sports is dumb."

"Tell me, what are your feelings on the English language?" Caleb asked dryly.

"Huh?" Will gave his father a blank look.

Julie cleared her throat, and gave Caleb a repressive look. This was no time to be worrying about Will's command of English. Or lack, thereof. Trying to focus on too many things at once would only confuse the child. And probably make him more uncooperative than he already was.

"If we could get started?" Julie said.

"This way," Caleb said as he headed toward the open French doors on the far side of the large recreation room.

"Is that one of them ret…things?" Will whispered to Julie.

"Yup," Julie whispered back.

They followed Caleb through the French doors onto a brick-paved terrace. There were large terra-cotta pots filled with multicolored flowers scattered around, and beneath the shade of a huge sugar maple tree was a glass-topped table with four wrought-iron chairs circling it. To the left of the French doors were several loungers with brightly flowered cushions. The whole scene radiated a sense of peace and tranquillity. It would be the perfect place to relax after a busy day.

"How lovely this is," Julie voiced her appreciation.

"He ain't got no swimming pool," Will pointed out. "At home, everybody's got a swimming pool."

"Everybody?" Julie set her briefcase down on the table and pulled out a pack of cards.

"Well, everybody who ain't poor," Will claimed. "Is you poor?" He shot the question at his father.

"Don't worry. I have enough money to pay the bills," Caleb said.

"Mom says that no one never has enough money. I have lots though. I gots me a trust fund from Mom's dad who died afor I was ever born. I don't mind sharing with you," Will offered.

"I appreciate the thought—" Caleb smiled at his son "—but you can't spend your money until you are of age."

"I got age, six years of age," Will insisted. "And Mom said I can spend my money just as I please."

"I am not your mother," Caleb said.

Not hardly, Julie thought with an appreciative glance at Caleb's very masculine body, her eyes lingering on his muscular forearms beneath the rolled-up sleeves of his pale blue denim shirt.

"But—" Will began.

"Shall we get started," Julie interrupted before the argument could escalate.

"Will, you sit there." She pointed to a chair.

Reluctantly Will sat down. "I hate tests."

"Really?" She sounded mildly curious. "If you haven't been to school, how do you know about tests?"

Will opened his mouth, closed it again and scowled at her.

"Please sit down there, Caleb," Julie said, hoping that having the distance of the table between them would help her to ignore him. It was a tactical error. Across from her, he was directly in her line of sight, and her eyes kept straying to him.

You are a teacher, she reprimanded herself. You are here to evaluate a child, not fantasize about the child's father.

"What's them?" Will pointed to the deck of cards she was holding.

"These are to test your ESP, because if you really are an alien in disguise then I can't teach you. Aliens are outside my area of expertise," Julie said seriously as she dealt ten of the cards facedown in front of him.

"Cool! Just like on *X-Files!*" Will scooted around on the chair in excitement. "Do you find many aliens?"

"Nary a one," Julie said.

"Aw, sh—"

"William Alister Tarrington!" Caleb bit out.

"What?" Will gave his father a confused look.

Julie looked from Caleb's furious features to Will's

confused ones and stifled a sigh. From the look on Will's face, she had the discouraging feeling that the boy had no clue as to why his father was so mad. It would appear there was a cultural gap a mile wide between father and son.

"I absolutely forbid——" Caleb began.

Julie hastily reached across the small table and touched Caleb's shoulder, intent only on stopping him before the whole situation exploded into anger on Caleb's part and tears on Will's, which would ruin any chance for her to evaluate the child today. Her fingers involuntarily twitched as she felt the warmth of his body beneath the soft cotton of his shirt.

Her touch felt like a live wire had been laid on Caleb's bare skin. It scorched his flesh and raced over his nerve endings, speeding up his heartbeat. He took a deep breath, hoping to regain control of his senses. It didn't work. The faint scent of the perfume she was wearing drifted into his lungs, deepening his sexual awareness of her.

Damn! Caleb thought with black humor. Of all times for his body to indulge in a sexual fantasy. When he was lecturing his son about inappropriate social behavior!

"Why can't I say sh—that word?" Will substituted at Caleb's glare. "Everybody says it. Mom does and all Mom's friends, and in the movies and——"

"What kind of movies do you see?" Caleb demanded.

"We seem to have wandered from the purpose of my visit," Julie interrupted, despite her sympathy for Caleb. He was really going to have his work cut out for him. Not only was the poor man going to have to try to forge some kind of relationship with a child he had never laid eyes on before two days ago, but he was also going to have to teach that child what was and wasn't allowed in normal society. A task that was bound to initially earn Will's resentment.

To Julie's relief, Caleb subsided without another word. Almost as if he was relieved to have her deal with the present problem.

Julie turned to Will. "I want you to close your eyes and concentrate on the number that is hidden on each of the ten cards. Tell me what you think each one is."

Will, with a cautious look at his father, obediently squeezed his eyes shut and caught his lower lip between his small teeth in concentration.

"The first one is six," Will decided.

"Am I right?" He opened one eye and peered hopefully at her.

"I'll tell you at the end," Julie said. "Guess the rest."

Will quickly guessed the remaining cards and then she flipped over the cards. "Aw, sh—damn!" he quickly amended.

"God give me strength," Caleb groaned.

"I guess I ain't no alien," Will lamented. "I only got two of the ten right."

"Oh, well, not everybody is lucky enough to be an alien," Julie sympathized.

"Yeah." Will looked morose for a second and then suddenly brightened. "Maybe I can get possessed."

Caleb grimaced. "Maybe you already—"

"Since you're a human, let's test some human skills," Julie hurriedly said. She didn't want Caleb giving Will ideas. The kid had enough already.

Handing Will a small beginning reader, she said, "Would you see if any of that looks familiar?"

Will opened the book and flipped through the pages.

"Nope," he finally said.

"No, what?" Julie, wise in the ways of kids, sought clarification.

"No, it don't look familiar. Ain't never seen it before," Will said.

"A literalist yet," Caleb said. "He sounds for all the world like his great-grandfather."

Will peered uncertainly at him. "I gots me a great-grandfather?"

"You had," Caleb said. "He died when I was a teenager. He was a judge, and you had to be really careful what you said to him because he took everything literally."

"A judge?" Will looked intrigued. "Did he hang anyone?"

Caleb chuckled, and the sound slipped through Julie's mind, soothing her sense of frustration at the way this session kept going off on tangents. Caleb had the most attractive chuckle. It made her feel warm and excited. As if something exhilarating was about to happen.

"Not that I know of," Caleb said. "Although he did threaten to horsewhip me the time I drove his car without permission."

"Really?" Will's eyes widened as he tried to imagine the scene.

"Can you read the book, Will?" Julie broke in.

"'Course I can," Will scoffed. "But I don't wanna. It's dumb."

"What do you like to read?" Julie asked.

"*Star Trek* books and *Goosebumps* and lots a'others."

"I see," Julie said slowly. "Unfortunately, I didn't bring anything like those with me."

"I gots a great book in my room. That guy that brought me here, he bought it for me in the airport to read on the plane," Will said. "Wanna see it?"

"Sure," Julie said.

Will jumped up and raced toward the house.

"What are those books he mentioned?" Caleb watched his son disappear through the French doors.

"Upper elementary level," Julie said slowly.

"Do you think he really can read them? I mean, he's never been to school."

"Did you notice the cards?" she asked.

"I didn't pay much attention. I assumed they were simply to break the ice. As far as I was concerned, he'd already melted it with his vocabulary," he said dryly.

"It does seem to be a bit on the X-rated side," she conceded. "But about those cards, Will remembered what he had guessed on all the cards. He didn't have to ask. Or even stop and think. And he didn't make a mistake."

"There were only ten cards," Caleb said.

"The average kid would be lucky to remember four of them."

Caleb frowned. "Meaning?"

"Meaning he has a good memory. A very good memory."

"I already knew that! He's apparently remembered every vulgarity he's ever heard."

"Here it is." Will burst through the French doors waving a ragged paperback. "It's a great book, all about a Jewish boy whose parents come to live in the

United States from Russia a long time ago. You wanna borrow it?'' he offered.

"Thanks.'' Julie accepted the book and tucked it into her briefcase.

"Have you ever tried writing a book yourself, Will?'' she asked.

"Nah,'' Will rejected the idea. "Printing's too hard. Them squiggly letters don't never come out right.''

"I see. How about math?'' Julie asked. "What are six and eight?''

Will shrugged. "Don't know. Ain't got my calculator.''

"Which would seem to be a powerful argument for learning to do sums in your head,'' Caleb observed.

"No, it ain't,'' Will said. "'Cause I ain't the one what wants to know. She does.'' He pointed a grubby finger at Julie. "She's the one what should learn to add.''

"Definitely the judge's offspring,'' Caleb muttered.

"But—'' Will started.

"Never mind,'' Julie cut him off. "I think I have a fair idea of what I wanted to know. Thanks for your help, Will.''

"You all done?'' Will looked surprised. "No more questions?''

"Nope. No more.''

"You coming back?'' Will eyed her hopefully. "Maybe we could try them cards again. Maybe I gots that ESP, but it's hidden deep.''

"Let's hope it stays hidden,'' Caleb muttered. "Will, I'm going to talk to Julie for a while. You go amuse yourself.''

Will obediently got to his feet and stood there look-ing at him.

"What is it?" Caleb asked.

"Where's my ten bucks?"

Caleb frowned. "What ten bu...dollars?"

"Mom always gives me ten bucks to go outside and amuse myself when she wants to talk to her dates."

Julie closed her eyes, praying the scorching heat she could feel burning its way over her cheekbones wasn't as visible as it felt. She had no doubt why his mother had given him the money to disappear. And it sure wasn't so she and her dates could talk.

She stole a quick glance at Caleb, but he looked more taken aback than angry at Will's inadvertent disclosure.

"I don't give bribes," Caleb finally said. "And I expect to be obeyed."

Will wrinkled his nose as he considered the situa-tion. "But I expects my ten bucks, and I ain't seeming to get it."

"There is a difference," Caleb said sternly. "I am the adult."

"All that means is that you done lived longer," Will retorted. "Someday I'll be as old as you."

"Not if you don't get out of here right this mo-ment!" Caleb snapped.

"Grown-ups!" Will grumbled as he stalked back into the house.

"I don't know what I'm going to do," Caleb mut-tered.

Julie studied Caleb's tense, frustrated features, not sure even in her own mind what to say to him. She liked Will and wanted to help him. But the trouble was, she also liked his father and that worried her.

"Caleb," she began slowly.

"Not here," Caleb cut her off. "He's probably eavesdropping."

"No, I ain't!" Will yelled from just inside the French doors.

Julie hastily swallowed the giggle threatening to escape. She had the distinct feeling from Caleb's harassed expression that he was not seeing the humor in the situation at the moment.

"Come on." Caleb got to his feet. "We'll go out for a cup of coffee. Away from little pitchers."

"Okay, but you'll have to drive. My car won't start, and I haven't had time to take it to the garage," Julie said, trying to tell herself that the pleasure she felt at his suggestion they go out for coffee was only because she could use the extra time to figure out how to phrase her refusal and not because she wanted to be alone with him. The problem was, she had never been very good at self-deception.

Chapter Three

Julie looked around with interest as Caleb pulled into the parking lot of a diner. The front of it was shaped like an old-fashioned trolley car, and it exuded a homey charm that appealed to her. But that it would appeal to Caleb surprised her. It was not at all the type of restaurant she would have expected a wealthy, sophisticated man like Caleb Tarrington to patronize.

"Coffee, please," Caleb told the waitress who appeared beside their booth the moment they sat down.

Julie studied his long, tanned fingers as they beat an impatient tattoo on the tabletop while he waited for their coffee to arrive. They were strong fingers, but it wasn't just physically that he was strong.

Caleb Tarrington was strong inside, where it really counted. In the character department. His dogged determination to do his best by his son was proof of that. His entire concentration had been on Will and how to best help him adjust to his new life.

The man deserved the truth from her.

"Thank you," Julie murmured absently as the waitress set her coffee down. But how much of the truth would be beneficial without discouraging him? she wondered.

"Spare me the euphemisms." Caleb seemed to read her mind with no difficulty. "Tell me what you think in plain English, not wrapped up in a lot of educational jargon or psychobabble."

"Okay, if the plain unvarnished truth is what you want, then it's what you'll get.

"First of all, I think your son has been neglected. Not physically, but emotionally and socially."

Caleb clamped his lips together as if holding back angry words, but who they were directed at, Julie didn't know. His ex-wife for what she had done to Will, or, more accurately, hadn't done, or herself for having the audacity to point it out.

"I figured that one out myself," Caleb finally said. "But that's past. It can't be changed. Now we need to devise a strategy for dealing with it."

Not *we*, Julie mentally corrected him. Caleb. She wasn't going to get involved.

"I will give you my input, but I have plans for the summer," Julie said.

"And your input is?" Caleb ignored the second part of her sentence.

"Based on my brief, my very brief, observation of your son, I would say that you have a two-pronged problem. The first and the easiest to deal with is his lack of necessary first-grade skills. It's a big plus that he reads well. Hopefully, his reading has brought him into contact with some of the history he should know."

"History!" Caleb's dark eyebrows arched in surprise. "In the first grade?"

"Definitely. Oh, we still do a few of the old-style social studies units on family and community, but we also give the kids a solid grounding in the history of the world and the United States."

"Don't you think you're pushing them a little? These are six-year-old kids, after all."

"Inquisitive six-year-old kids. Giving them a sense of history early is crucial.

"But that's a side issue," she said. "Scholastically, Will's most pressing need would appear to be bringing his writing and math skills up to speed. I don't anticipate much of a problem because he seems to be a very bright little boy.

"However, his social skills..." Julie paused, mentally searching for a diplomatic way of saying it.

"You mean his language would send any suburban soccer mom running for her four-wheel drive?" Caleb said bluntly.

Julie sighed. "Unfortunately that's exactly what I mean. But even worse than his colorful language is that he doesn't seem to realize that he shouldn't say...the things he does."

Caleb smiled ruefully. "He's more amoral than immoral?"

"Got it in one! Which unfortunately is going to make the job that much harder."

Caleb frowned, and Julie watched as a muscle in the corner of his mouth twitched with the strength of the emotions he was holding in check. Seeing Caleb angry would be a formidable sight, Julie thought with an inward shudder. She wouldn't care to have that anger directed at her.

"Why harder?" Caleb asked.

"Because if Will knew that the words he used were…"

"Bad?" Caleb filled in.

"No!" Julie vehemently shook her head, and Caleb watched in fascination as the light-brown strands brushed the velvety skin of her cheeks. Her hair looked so soft and silky.

He wondered what it would feel like to leisurely run his fingers through it. To have the curly ends brush against his bare skin. He swallowed uneasily as his body began to react to the images flooding his mind. With an effort, he wrenched his thoughts back to what she was saying and not what she looked like.

"Words in and of themselves are not bad." Julie insisted. "It's people's reactions to them that cause the trouble. Most kids learn very early which words get a rise out of their parents, and they tend to save those words to use on the playground to try to impress the other kids with how daring they are."

"But Will isn't being daring," Caleb said. "He's simply repeating what he thinks is normal."

"Exactly. You're going to have to teach him to substitute more acceptable words."

"How am I supposed to do that? I can't stand over him twenty-four hours a day and correct his English."

Julie chuckled at the image Caleb's words evoked.

Caleb momentarily forgot his growing sense of impending disaster at the enchanting sound of her laughter. It trickled through his mind, lightening his mood, and making him believe that he really could cope with his son's problems.

"Maybe if I found Will a playmate or two from among my friends' sons," Caleb said thoughtfully.

"Bad idea," Julie vetoed. "At least, initially. Kids being kids, Will is far more likely to teach his language to them than learn to suppress it because they don't use it."

"You think so?" Caleb asked doubtfully.

"I know so," Julie said firmly. "And I also know that the mothers' reaction will be to refuse to allow their sons to play with Will, which will effectively isolate him. And social isolation is a recipe for a very unhappy childhood. Give him a month to get used to not using objectionable words, and then you can find him a couple of playmates."

"I suppose—" Caleb broke off as the cell phone in his pocket rang. "Excuse me, I'd better get this," he said. "It could be Miss Vincent about Will."

Julie leaned back against the vinyl cushion as he answered the call. It quickly became apparent that the caller wasn't his housekeeper. From the totally incomprehensible conversation Caleb was carrying on about stress mass, she guessed the call was work-related.

She watched him as he talked, fascinated by the way he gestured with his hands to make a point. Caleb Tarrington was the most physically compelling man she had ever met. There was something about the sum of his parts that appealed to her on an instinctive level as no other man ever had.

Intellectual attraction she could understand and deal with. But how on earth could she reason with the breathless excitement that flooded her every time she looked at him? She had no idea because her reaction defied logic.

"I'll get back to you as soon as I can, Ben." Caleb

concluded his call, switched the phone off and put it back in his pocket.

For a long moment, he studied the gray tabletop as if marshaling his arguments, and then he looked up. His blue gaze caught and held hers.

"Julie, I need your help. Will needs your help."

Julie instinctively shook her head.

"Please don't refuse until you've heard me out."

"All right." Julie agreed more because she didn't know what else to say. The truth was certainly not an option. She could just imagine his reaction if she were to say, "So sorry, Caleb, but I can't help your son because I want to throw my arms around you and kiss you senseless, and it scares me. It scares me because I've never felt like this before."

Not only that, but it was a feeling that most emphatically didn't fit into her plans. She already had her future neatly mapped out. In seven or eight years, she intended to find a nice, pleasant man with whom she could build a marriage. A fellow educator who shared her love of teaching and wouldn't expect her to give it up to play housewife. A man who would be content with one child and would be an equal partner in raising him. A man who would be willing to accept the role she gave him in her life, not try to take it over.

As she very strongly suspected Caleb would do. The very intensity of his personality would preclude the kind of warm, companionable relationship she intended to settle for. Julie frowned slightly as she realized the word she'd chosen. She wasn't settling for anything, she mentally refuted her subconscious's choice of words. That was the type of relationship she wanted. There was no room in her life for a mad, passionate love affair in or out of marriage.

Besides, she thought with a complete lack of self-deception, chance would be a fine thing. She wasn't the type of woman who inspired thoughts of unbridled lust in men. All the men she'd ever known had either seen her as the girl-next-door or as the kid sister they'd never had. Even Caleb. She remembered his comment about her looking too young to have graduated from college. Men didn't whisper sweet nothings in her ear. They told her about the women they were in love with in mind-numbing detail and asked her advice on how to catch them.

"Please listen," Caleb responded to her frown, thinking it was in reaction to his request and not her own thoughts.

"I said I would, and I will," Julie said, "but that's all I'm promising."

"If you will tutor Will and help me figure out how to muzzle his language, you can name your price," Caleb said.

"This isn't a job that can be totally delegated to a tutor," Julie said, trying to make him understand the necessity of his being personally involved. "Will is your son, and he needs you."

"I know he's my son, but until two days ago I hadn't even met him. I had no idea when I set up my work schedule last year that I would have him living with me."

"Change your work schedule," Julie said flatly.

Caleb ran his fingers through his short dark hair in frustration.

"It isn't that easy. I not only have to finalize the plans for a shopping center, but the preliminary plans for the renovation of the high school are also due at the end of next month. Both of them have to be turned in on time because contractors and builders are lined up to act on them. If I cause a delay, it's going to cost a lot of people a lot of money. Some of whom can ill afford to lose it."

"Even without the financial consideration, the kids need that high school fixed," Julie conceded. "The old one is falling down around their ears."

"Just the ceiling tiles," Caleb said. "And to further complicate matters, Miss Andrews, my secretary, had to leave town last week with no warning because her mother had a heart attack. At the moment, her mother's in the hospital, and Miss Andrews has no idea when she'll be able to return."

"Miss Andrews?" Julie's voice rose questioningly. She'd done temporary work in dozens of offices while she was in college and in every one of them the boss had been on a first-name basis with his secretary.

"I was lucky enough to find Miss Andrews when I moved back from California six and a half years ago and first opened my office. She's been with me ever since. She's a treasure. I'd be lost without her."

"I see," Julie muttered, her curiosity about the woman still unfilled. "Maybe you could involve your..." She gestured ineffectively as if trying to pluck an appropriate word out of the air. Caleb seemed far too sophisticated to have something as juvenile-sounding as a girlfriend.

"Significant other," she finally chose, "in Will's lessons. If you're going to present Will with a stepmother, this would be a good chance for them to get acquainted. She could handle most of the actual tutoring with a little direction. At his level, all that's really needed is someone with patience and time.''

Julie unconsciously held her breath, waiting for his response.

"I don't have a significant other," Caleb said flatly. "My one trip down the aisle cured me of all those idiotic notions of true love and happily-ever-after. Marriage is nothing more than sex with the blessings of the legal system.''

Julie blinked at such a comprehensive dismissal of the fundamental unit of civilization.

"It also has the blessings of the Church," she finally said.

"Don't tell me you believe that Prince Charming is going to ride out of the sunset and carry you off to live happily ever after?'' Caleb sneered.

"You're confused. Prince Charming doesn't ride out of the sunset, he rides into it. But to answer your question, no, I am not waiting for Prince Charming. I am perfectly aware that it wouldn't do me any good.''

"Why not?" Caleb asked, curious at the way her mind worked. If ever there was a woman who looked as if she belonged in a fairy tale it was Julie Raffet. But not cast as Cinderella, Caleb decided as he studied the surprisingly firm line of her small chin. She might be physically small, but he suspected her spirit was big enough for any challenge. She'd never allow herself to be taken advantage of by a bunch of ugly stepsisters. She'd give them a piece of her mind and march out of the house to find her own way.

"Haven't you ever noticed that the heroines of fairy tales are always beautiful?'' Unconsciously, her voice took on a wistful note.

"But we seem to have wandered rather far from the point," she said, returning to the subject of Will.

"Julie." Caleb looked at her, and Julie found her gaze caught and held by the tiny lights she could see gleaming in the depths of his eyes. "The most important point is that you can make a big difference in Will's life. Please, help him."

His plea battered at her resistance.

With effort, she tore her eyes from his compelling stare and looked down into her coffee cup. She couldn't think when she was looking at him. Other thoughts, thoughts that had nothing to do with tutoring, kept intruding.

She tried to consider the situation objectively. She knew if Caleb had been an unattractive man who left her cold emotionally, she would have agreed to help Will in a second. What was stopping her was Caleb himself. She stole a surreptitious glance at him to find him studying her intently.

No, she corrected herself. What was stopping her was her compulsive, mindless attraction to him.

That was what worried her. That her sexual attraction would deepen if she was around him for any length of time. But would it? Could sexual attraction grow when neither party was feeding it? And they wouldn't. She had better sense, and he quite clearly had no desire to get himself entangled in another male-female relationship. Logically her intense attraction should die a natural death from lack of encouragement. And she'd planned her whole life logically. It was a little late to abandon an approach that had served her so well.

She'd do it, she finally decided, ignoring the sudden spurt of excitement she felt at her decision.

But she'd be wise to get Caleb's agreement to a few matters first, her sense of practicality asserted itself.

"I'll tutor Will on a couple of conditions."

Her stomach twisted at the brilliance of his relieved smile.

"First, our school parents' group is going to raise money next year to replace the antiquated playground equipment. I want you to offer to design it for them for free. That will save a substantial amount of money."

"You help Will, and I'll *give* them the playground," Caleb promised.

To his surprise, Julie shook her head. "No, thanks. If they raise the money for the equipment themselves, they'll feel a sense of ownership that they won't have if the playground is just handed to them. Designing it will be plenty."

"My firm has a specialist who does all our playgrounds. I'll have her do it."

"You won't do it yourself?" Julie felt a stab of dismay. She'd had some vague idea of seeing him around the school while he was working on it.

"Not won't. Can't. Because of all the government regulations on the construction and landscaping of playgrounds. I don't know them. Melissa does. She won't accidentally make a costly mistake."

"All right, we'll accept her help."

"You said a 'couple of things,'" Caleb said slowly, wondering what else she wanted. With anyone else, he would have assumed a hefty tutoring fee, but with this woman he simply didn't know.

So far, Julie Raffet's personality had defied easy categorization. In all areas. She looked fragile enough to break, and yet she had an iron determination that he suspected rivaled his own. And, according to what John had said, she was a highly trained, highly competent professional. And when you added to that the fact that she really seemed to like kids, not just see them as objects to be whipped into shape, you had an intriguing bundle of feminine characteristics.

"I want you to involve yourself in Will's lessons," she told him.

"But I already told you about my schedule," Caleb said.

"We'll figure out a way around the problem. But there is no way around the fact that you're his father. You need to get to know him. He needs to learn to see you as an authority figure."

"I don't think the kid even knows what an authority figure is!" Caleb grumbled. "Tell me, do you have any ideas on how to arrange things at work or is that my department?"

He wasn't really surprised to find that she did have a specific suggestion.

"I worked as a temp in lots of offices during college," she said. "How about if I give you a hand in the office in the mornings until your Miss Andrews is able to come back? That should free up some of your time."

"It might work," Caleb said thoughtfully. "You could handle a lot of the routine paperwork and keep the interruptions to a minimum. If you were to help in the mornings, and I worked at home at night, I could spend my afternoons with Will."

"Then we have a deal," Julie said, having the oddest feeling that she'd just surrendered far more than a few weeks of her summer.

"We have a deal." Caleb repeated the words like a vow. "Now that that's settled, let's go take a look at your car." He dropped some bills on the table beside his empty coffee cup and got to his feet.

"My car?" she repeated blankly.

"Sure. You helped me out this morning. I'd like to return the favor and help you."

"Can you?" Julie asked curiously.

"Can I what?" He held the door open for her with an old-fashioned courtesy she found enchanting. In a lot of ways, Caleb seemed to have wandered straight out of one of those fairy tales he was so disparaging about.

"Tell what's wrong with my car by looking at it?" she answered him once they were in his car.

"Probably," he said. "When I was a teenager, my ambition was to be a race-car driver. I was always taking engines apart."

"I can take an engine apart. It's putting it back together again that's the trick," she said dryly.

"Oh, ye of little faith." He gave her a grin that made her heart pound. Suddenly, the morning seemed clearer, more in focus than it had before. As if being around Caleb somehow fine-tuned her world.

"Where do you live?" he asked as he started his car.

"My place is over in back of the old junior-high-school building, 1282 Mylart Street."

Caleb pulled into the traffic with an easy competence she admired.

"I know the area," he said.

Julie spent the short ride home wondering how Caleb knew the area. It certainly wasn't the kind of neighborhood she would have expected him to be acquainted with. The houses were solidly working-class, and to the best of her knowledge not a single one of them boasted an interesting architectural feature. Nor did anyone live in the neighborhood whom Caleb would be likely to know socially.

"Third house on the right," she said once he'd turned onto her street.

Caleb pulled up in front of her neat little bungalow.

"Sears," he announced.

Julie looked around for a clue to his comment and when she didn't find one asked, "What about Sears?"

"You have a Sears house. Didn't they tell you when they bought it?" He climbed out of the car and walked toward the house, studying it with a professional eye.

"No." Julie followed him.

"Original siding," he noted.

"Sure is. I sunk every penny I had into the down payment when I bought it this spring. Any improvements will have to wait a couple of years. And what is an original Sears house?"

"Sears and Roebuck used to sell house kits. They would ship the whole thing to the buyer, and he would have it assembled on his lot. They were very popular at one time. This is one of the smaller models."

"Really?" Julie was intrigued by his disclosure. "My little house came from a catalog?"

"Uh-huh. Although…" He paused as he rounded the side of the house. "Sears wouldn't have had anything to do with that." He gestured toward the ramshackle single-car garage. "It doesn't look safe."

"It's safe enough to store my gardening equipment, which is all I use it for."

"You should tear it down before it falls down on your head."

"Don't exaggerate."

"I never exaggerate," he retorted. "If anything, I've understated the case. It leans to the right."

"So does the Leaning Tower of Pisa, and people travel from all over the world to see it," she said smugly.

"That's what you came to see." She pointed to the fifteen-year-old Buick sitting in the driveway. "That's Palladin. He is definitely not feeling well."

Caleb walked over to the car. Somehow, he wasn't the least bit surprised to find that she called the car Palladin. Julie Raffet wasn't the kind of woman to call her car anything as mundane as Betsy.

"Poor Palladin." She patted the car's dusty hood. "We've been through a lot together. He was my very first car. Dad paid half, and I paid the other half."

"Reach inside and release the hood catch, will you?" Caleb asked.

Julie did, and then joined him as he bent over the engine. Surreptitiously, she studied his intent features.

For a moment she savored the way the sun gilded his skin before she focused on the network of tiny lines etched into his skin at the corners of his eyes. As if he smiled a lot. Or grimaced a lot. She forced herself to face the fact that she didn't really know enough about Caleb Tarrington to decide which it was.

"...start?"

Julie blinked as she suddenly realized that he'd asked her something.

"I'm sorry," she muttered. "What did you say?"

Wonderful, he thought. Julie Raffet was so bored with his company that she couldn't even bring herself to pay attention to what he was saying. The knowledge depressed him, and the fact that he even cared depressed him even more.

Julie Raffet was his son's tutor. And that was all she was, he told himself. That was all she would ever be. A vibrant woman like her would never look at a rather staid man burdened with the baggage of a failed marriage and a small son.

"I asked for a key to start the car," he repeated.

"A key?" she repeated, trying to remember where she'd left it. She should have left it in the car, she thought with hindsight. No one was going to steal a car that wouldn't start.

"It's in the house," she finally said.

"I'll come with you," Caleb said. He was very curious about what kind of home she had created for herself.

He followed her across the neatly trimmed lawn to the wide front porch, waiting while she fished her house key out of her pocket and unlocked the door.

As he walked inside, he was enveloped in the most delightful smell. His large nose wrinkled appreciatively. Her house smelled of... He searched his mind trying to identify the aroma and couldn't. The closest he could come was floral.

"Too strong?" Julie noticed his reaction.

"I like it. What is it?"

"Potpourri. I'm experimenting with making my own. I..." She paused as she noticed the red blinking light on her answering machine. "Excuse me a second while I check my message."

She pushed the play button and a second later a deep male voice filled the room.

"Sweetheart, it's me, Joe. I'm desperate. I need

your help. Fast. By tonight at the latest. Call me and tell me what turns you on.''

Caleb's eyes widened as the sudden jolt of some emotion he couldn't quite label tore through him. Who was the guy who'd left the message? Why was he calling Julie sweetheart, and why did he want to know what turned her on?

Caleb studied Julie's pensive face, wondering what she was thinking. She appeared to be more curious than anything else, he finally decided. Or maybe she was simply intrigued by the guy's approach. He hoped not. She deserved more finesse than that from the men in her life. The caller, whoever he was, had all the charm of a bulldozer and about as much subtlety.

Caleb searched his mind for a way to ask Julie what her relationship with the man was but came up blank. Their own relationship didn't extend to him asking her about the men in her life. Actually it didn't extend to any personal questions. The thought deepened his sense of irritation.

He watched as she deleted the message and turned back to him. Apparently she didn't feel the message warranted an immediate answer. The knowledge soothed him somewhat.

Julie surreptitiously looked around the living room. The car key wasn't in plain sight.

Damn! she thought in annoyance. Why couldn't she ever remember where she'd left her key? She didn't want Caleb to think she was absentminded.

"Can I have the car key?" he asked.

"Just a minute," she stalled. "I'm thinking."

"About whether you're going to let me have it?''

"No." She gave up stalling and told him the truth, "About which safe place I put it in."

"The last one."

"What?" She peered uncertainly at him.

"It's always in the last place you look."

"Thank you, Albert Einstein!"

Caleb's mouth lifted in an infectious smile. "You're welcome."

Julie grinned back, warmed by the fact that he didn't make any snide cracks about forgetfulness.

"When was the last time you had the key?" he asked.

Julie frowned slightly, thinking. "Two days ago. When I came home from school. I parked in the driveway and came in through the kitchen."

She went into the kitchen and looked around. The car key was sitting in the middle of her small, maple kitchen table.

"Voilà," she announced.

"Good, let's go give it a try." Caleb headed toward the back door.

Once they reached the car, he leaned over the engine while Julie got into the car.

"Start it up," he told Julie.

Julie obediently turned the key. The car made its by-now-familiar grinding noise, but didn't start.

"How old is your battery?" Caleb's voice sounded muffled to her.

Julie slipped out of the car and joined him, curious about what he was studying so intently. She moved closer and looked at the engine. Closer didn't help. It still looked like a greasy, incomprehensible pile of metal to her.

"Just a few months old," she said.

Caleb looked up, and his gaze caught hers. Instantly, all thoughts of cars and batteries were washed away by the swirling depths of her dark brown eyes.

"It can't be the battery," she said, and to Caleb's ears, her voice seemed to be coming from a long way off.

"Probably not," he muttered, struggling to pull himself free of the sensual spell she was so effortlessly weaving around him.

"Maybe your car has a loose connection," he finally said.

Maybe he was the one with a loose connection, he thought wryly. That was the only explanation that he could think of for his preoccupation with a woman who treated him in the same casual manner that she treated his son.

His eyes lingered on the soft fullness of her mouth. Encouragement or not, he wanted to kiss her. He wanted to see if her lips really were as soft as they looked. He wanted to inhale the scent of her skin as he tacitly explored it.

Caleb felt the air in his chest expanding beneath the intensity of longing. She was so close to him. All he had to do would be to lean forward ever so slightly. Just a few inches and their lips would meet. A few inches and he could...

Julie shifted slightly, and her movement momentarily shook him free from the sensuality he was drowning in. What on earth was the matter with him? he wondered uneasily. He was reacting to Julie Raffet like a teenager in the throes of an adolescent hormone attack. Just as he had reacted to Murna.

The memory of his first wife effectively doused his ardor as nothing else could have.

He'd been there and done that, he thought grimly, and it had been a disaster from start to finish. He knew the dangers of giving in to sexual curiosity. No one knew it better.

The problem was remembering the bitterly learned lesson when he was around Julie Raffet. But he could do it, he assured himself. He was a rational human being who was in control of his emotions. His emotions didn't control him.

Determinedly, he turned back to his study of the engine.

Julie shivered, feeling a distinct sense of loss. Don't be an idiot, she told herself. You haven't lost anything. Caleb Tarrington hadn't had any intention of kissing her. He'd simply been close to her, and her imagination had immediately leaped to a conclusion. If he hadn't been turned on by her beautiful sister, he sure wasn't going to find her attractive. The humiliating knowledge stiffened her spine.

"I have some car tools in the trunk. Should I get them?" Julie asked, proud of the evenness of her voice.

"I don't think I'll need them," he murmured. "I think the problem is this loose wire. Try starting it now."

Julie slipped behind the seat and turned the key. The car gave an asthmatic cough, sputtered once and finally came to life.

"Thanks," Julie told him as she got out of the car.

"It's the least I could do," he said.

And what would be the most he could do? Julie wondered on a sudden surge of excitement. He could...

"We'll start Will's tutoring tomorrow," he said.

"It'll have to be the day after tomorrow," she said. "Tomorrow I have an interview for a teaching position at that new charter school they're opening up on the north side of town this fall."

Caleb stiffened as her words jarred loose bitter memories of his ex-wife's total absorption in her career. Once again he and his son were being relegated to second place behind a woman's career.

"Fine." His clipped acceptance sounded anything but fine to Julie.

"I'll see you the day after tomorrow then," he said coldly, and without another word he turned on his heel and left.

Julie watched him get into his car and drive away without a backward glance.

What was that all about? she wondered in confusion. Surely he couldn't be all that upset about a one-day delay. Not when she had a valid reason. An important reason. Important to her and important to all the kids she hoped to teach at the new school.

She had no idea why Caleb had reacted as he had, and the reason she had no idea was that she knew almost nothing about Caleb Tarrington, she reminded herself. It was even possible that his abrupt departure had had nothing to do with her announcement. And it was also possible that Prince Charming really would ride into her life and sweep her off her feet. Possible. But about as probable as her winning the lottery.

Chapter Four

Julie glanced from the gleaming brass office directory to the right of the bank of elevators and then back to the slip of paper on which she'd jotted down the address Caleb had left on her answering machine yesterday while she'd been at her interview. The information didn't match. The directory said that Caleb Tarrington and Associates was on the fifth floor, but the office number Caleb had given her was on the seventh floor.

She frowned thoughtfully as she entered the waiting elevator. She'd try the seventh floor first under the assumption that Caleb surely knew where he worked, she decided. He hadn't struck her as the least bit vague or uncertain.

She shivered slightly as she remembered the purposeful gleam in his eyes when he'd been trying to convince her to tutor Will. He'd radiated a feeling of confident competence.

Would he radiate that same kind of confidence

when he made love to a woman? she wondered. Would he take a woman in his arms and hold her with assurance? Would he...

Julie's fanciful speculation was interrupted when the elevator doors opened with a dignified chime on the seventh floor. And a good thing too, she assured herself. Daydreaming about Caleb Tarrington was not going to help her get over her unwanted attraction to him. Being realistic was. She swallowed uneasily as she remembered the warmth of his large body as they'd both bent over her car's engine. Actually, things didn't get more realistic than Caleb Tarrington's physical presence, she conceded.

Determinedly, Julie shoved her thoughts to the back of her mind and went in search of suite 7C. She found it three doors down on the right. Pausing in front of the door, she straightened the front of her severely tailored green suit, ran her fingers over the smooth sweep of her chignon to make sure no wayward strands of hair had escaped and then, hoping her appearance compared favorably with the revered Miss Andrews, pushed open the door.

To find herself in a large empty reception room. Directly in front of her was a cherry desk piled high with papers. Behind it were filing cabinets. Several of the cabinet drawers had been pulled open and left that way. Discarded files had been tossed on top of the cabinets.

Julie walked over to the desk and picked up one of the files that littered it. It was labeled Tarrington and Associates.

"This must be the place," she muttered. "And it's definitely the time." So where was Caleb Tarrington?

As if in answer to her question, the door to the

right of the desk burst open, and Caleb stalked into the room. He had a file clutched in one hand and a frustrated expression on his face.

"Why are you up here and your company offices are listed two floors below?" Julie hurried into speech as if the sound of her voice could somehow extinguish the excitement fountaining through her at the sight of him.

"So you came," he grumbled.

"As promised," Julie answered, wondering what had put him in a bad mood so early in the morning. She wanted to smooth out the annoyed lines in his face with her fingers. She wanted to... Act like a secretary, Julie hastily stifled her imagination.

"But that doesn't answer my question." She made an effort to focus on a safe, impersonal subject. "Why are you up here, and your office is listed as downstairs?"

"So I can get some work done." He pitched the folder he was holding on top of the pile of papers on the desk. It teetered for a moment, and then succumbed to the law of gravity and slid to the floor. Caleb ignored it.

"When I was down in the main office with the rest of the staff, they came running to me with every little problem. When I'm not there, they solve their own problems, or else they save them up for me to deal with at our weekly meetings."

"An efficient solution," Julie agreed. "Which is a lot more than can be said for your filing methods." She rescued the folder on the floor.

"If you had been here yesterday..." Caleb began.

"Well, I wasn't. I was at my interview, and it was fantastic."

Caleb felt his chest tighten beneath the brilliance of her smile. She looked as if she'd won the lottery. Clearly she hadn't any regrets about putting him off for a day.

"You wouldn't believe what they are planning to do at the new charter school, Caleb," she enthused. "Or the freedom the teachers are going to have to work with the kids."

Caleb watched the sparkles swirling in the depths of her eyes and felt an answering tug of emotion. It was just intellectual curiosity, he assured himself. Now that he had a son to educate, it was normal for him to be interested in the educational process.

"What do you mean, freedom?" he asked. "It seems to me that a teacher has lots of freedom. There's just you and the kids in the classroom. You can do anything you want."

Julie grimaced. "Allow me to disabuse you of that notion. In my school we have to cover a set number of pages of material in each subject each day. Never mind if the kids need more time to learn a particular concept, if it's Friday, we'd better be on page fifty-two or the principal will have my head."

"And this new school will change all that?" Caleb asked, taken aback by the picture she was painting. He'd had no idea that elementary schools were so regimented.

"Oh yes!" Julie launched into a glowing account of teaching techniques she'd be able to try out.

Since he didn't have the background to even begin to understand what she was talking about, Caleb simply focused on the warm, melodious sound of her voice. The happy cadence of her voice lifted his spirits. It flowed over him, soothing his hypertense muscles and washing away his sense of living in a war zone caused by trying to keep the peace between his housekeeper and his son.

If just the sound of her voice could do that, what would happen if he were to kiss her? he wondered.

In unconscious response to the tantalizing thought, his eyes dropped to her soft lips, and a longing that was so intense it was almost painful tore through him. Don't go there, his intellect told him, but the warning was faint and far-off. No match at all for the temptation of her lips.

Julie's voice trailed away as she noticed the faintly glazed expression in Caleb's bright blue eyes. As if he was bored to death. And he probably was, she conceded fairly. Not everyone found various teaching techniques as enthralling as she did. In fact, most of her friends accused her of carrying a soapbox around with her so she could mount it at the drop of a hat. But despite the teasing, they all listened politely.

Caleb's response was different. Was he not bothering to listen because he wasn't her friend? The thought made her feel faintly panicky, even though she knew it was an irrational reaction. Caleb Tarrington was the parent of a child she was tutoring. That was all he was. Friendship didn't come into it.

"But enough about my interview." Julie made an effort to focus on why she was actually here. "Why don't you give me an overview of how your office works."

"My office?" Caleb repeated blankly.

Maybe she needed to go back and reread one of those magazine articles that told you how to talk to men, Julie thought ruefully. Because she sure wasn't managing to communicate with this one.

"Your office," she repeated.

"Yes, the office." Caleb dragged his mind back to mundane matters with an effort.

"It's really very simple," he said, launching into an explanation of how the office normally operated and what role the absent Miss Andrews filled.

Julie's self-confidence grew as she listened. The work Caleb did was different from anything she'd handled before, but an office was an office, and the work involved was pretty much the same no matter what the profession. She would be able to handle it with a minimum of problems, she decided.

"Do you only have hard-copy files?" She looked askance at the mess on the desk. "Or are all those backed up on the computer?" Julie gestured toward the computer setup on the stand beside the desk.

"Miss Andrews insists on putting everything in the computer, but I like paper. Things get lost in the computer," Caleb complained.

"Nothing ever gets lost in the computer," she said. "It's all there, the trick is getting it out."

"A useful trick if you've mastered it. Have you?" he asked curiously. Julie Raffet was turning out to be a whole lot more than just a very talented teacher.

"Mostly. I spent one semester working in the office of a man who taught computer seminars for businesses. I picked up a lot of useful information.

"Where do you keep your supplies?" she asked.

"Through here." Caleb headed toward the door opposite his own office, and Julie followed him. It led to a small storeroom.

Caleb pulled open the door to the room's closet and gestured into its depths. "This is where Miss Andrews keeps everything."

Julie stepped around Caleb into the large closet and looked over the well-stocked shelves. Things appeared to have been jumbled together in a totally random manner.

"Usually Miss Andrews keeps things neater than this." Caleb felt some explanation was called for. "But yesterday I was looking for something I needed.

Julie smiled at his sheepish expression. "I take it you didn't find it?"

Caleb watched, fascinated at the enchanting way her lips curved at the corners.

"No, I didn't," he conceded. "I had to call downstairs and have them send some fax paper up. Which reminds me, I need some drafting pencils."

He reached around her and pushed aside a stack of typing paper on the top shelf.

The spicy scent of his cologne enveloped her, and she swallowed uneasily. He smelled delicious. Almost edible.

"I'm sure I saw a box of them here yesterday." His voice as he searched the back of the shelf, sounded muffled. Not that she cared. Mere words couldn't begin to compete with the compulsive lure of his body.

"I knew I'd seen them!" Caleb triumphantly yanked a box off the shelf. Unfortunately, his action dislodged a box of paper clips.

Julie automatically reached for the falling box at the same time Caleb did. She collided with him and, completely thrown off balance by the sensations that engulfed her, tried to retreat. Her foot hit something lying on the floor, and she tripped.

Caleb instinctively grabbed her and pulled her up against his body to steady her.

Julie barely managed to suppress a shocked gasp as she felt the pressure of his arms around her. Her skin began to tingle, sparking her nerves to life. She could feel the hardness of his chest against her much softer breasts. It was a difference she longed to explore.

This was all wrong! Julie's subconscious struggled to bring her to her senses. She knew she shouldn't revel in the feel of his body, but, try as she might, she couldn't quite remember why. How could touching him be wrong? It felt so good. So right to be this close to him.

"Sorry, I...um..." Caleb's voice trailed away as he scrambled to remember what he was sorry for. Certainly not for having her in his arms. He hadn't meant to drop those clips. Nor had he planned to embrace her, but now that he had...

A hard thump on his shoulder broke into his muddled thoughts, and he blinked in confusion, wondering for a moment if Julie had hit him.

A second later the entire contents of the top shelf came cascading down over them and, as he gathered her closer to protect her from the falling debris, he realized what must have happened. His pulling out the box of drafting pencils had disturbed the precarious balance of the remaining supplies, causing everything to fall. And he should be grateful for the interruption, he tried to tell himself. If it hadn't happened, he might have given in to the temptation and kissed her. Despite knowing that it was a bad idea.

Apprehensively, he looked at Julie to find her eyeing him uncertainly. As if she was puzzled by his behavior. And it was no wonder, he thought in self-disgust. What kind of man took advantage of a woman tripping to try to satisfy his own urge to touch her?

A normal man, Caleb answered his own question. At least they did if the woman in question was as appealing as Julie Raffet was. But this was not a normal sort of circumstances, he grimly reminded himself. Julie was doing him a big favor. Two, in fact. And if he didn't want her to walk out on him and Will, he had to convince her that she was safe with him. As safe as if she were his sister.

No, he mentally jettisoned the comparison. There as no way on earth he could ever think of Julie as a relative. But maybe as a friend. He latched onto the idea with a feeling of desperation. Or even better as the fiancée of his best friend. Someone who was strictly off limits. Maybe he could do that.

Julie stepped back, and an intense feeling of loss filled him. As if something of infinite value had just slipped out of his grasp.

"What a mess."

Julie's voice sounded strange to him. Was she furious at him for taking advantage of the situation to hold her?

"Um, I didn't mean to grab you like that." He tried to placate her in case she was. "I mean, I didn't expect... I certainly wouldn't have... But when you tripped..."

With a profound sense of loss, Julie listened to his garbled attempt to rationalize away the exquisite feelings she'd discovered in his arms. What did you expect, you idiot, she berated herself. That he would say that he found holding you the defining moment in his life? Get real. He's a very sophisticated man. Holding a woman in his arms probably didn't even register as

Retreating into improbable daydreams was definitely not the answer. She forced her eyes open, rejecting the temptation. Daydreaming about a man was something she'd outgrown years ago. Now she was an adult. Now she dealt with the world the way it was and not the way she wanted it to be. And the reality was that men in general, and Caleb in particular, didn't see her as sexy. As the object of their desire. Caleb's embarrassing haste to make sure she hadn't misread his actions was proof of that.

And that being the case, all she could do was make a determined effort to treat Caleb with the same casual friendship she treated all the men she knew.

Julie sighed as she started to pick up the mess on the floor. It wasn't going to be easy, but it was the only viable option she could see.

As the morning wore on, Julie discovered that Caleb hadn't been exaggerating when he'd said that he was busy. Not only had the phone rung nonstop, but several people had arrived to consult with him about various projects.

When a member of the school board called shortly before noon insisting on a meeting that afternoon, Julie had worried that Caleb might agree and send her home to work with Will by herself. But to her relief, he had refused. And when the woman had insisted, Caleb had flatly told her that his afternoon was booked solid and she could either make an appointment for the next morning or else send him a letter outlining her concerns.

At exactly noon, Caleb stuck his head out of his office and announced, "Five minutes and we're out of here."

"Can do," Julie announced to the empty space where he had been.

She hit the save button on the computer then put the folder she'd been copying into her desk drawer to finish tomorrow.

Caleb reappeared five minutes later to find Julie waiting by the door.

"Good Lord, a woman who's on time?" he said, rather surprised not to have to wait for her. During his brief marriage, he couldn't remember Murna ever being on time. For anything.

"Good Lord, a man spouting stereotyped drivel!" Julie retorted.

"Things become stereotyped because they are true," he defended himself.

"I've heard that theory before, and it sounds like just more stereotyping to me."

"Sounds more like a circular argument to me," Caleb said. "But never mind. Let's get out of here while the coast is clear."

Leaning around her, he pushed open the door. The faint spicy scent that she was coming to associate with Caleb drifted into her lungs, making her remember earlier this morning when she'd smelled that same scent from so much closer. Making her remember what it had felt like when he'd...

Don't go there! She hauled herself up short. Forget what happened in the past. Concentrate on the present. That's where life is lived. All anyone ever had was the present.

"You can follow me home," Caleb said as he pushed the down button on the elevator.

"Sorry, I haven't got my jogging shoes. My car is at the garage getting the once-over."

Caleb frowned. "It died again?"

"No, but I figured that as long as I had it running I should take it down to the garage and let them do whatever it is that garages do to cars. What garages very *slowly* do to cars," she amended. "I took it in after my interview yesterday, and they promised faithfully they'd have it done by this morning."

Caleb smiled at her disgruntled expression. "If you believed that, I've got a bridge I want to sell you."

Julie grimaced. "It was rather credulous of me, wasn't it? But they're usually reliable. If they weren't, I would have gone to the grocery store before I took the car in instead of planning on doing it after."

"An easily fixed problem. We'll stop at the store on the way home."

"But I need milk and frozen stuff."

"I do have a refrigerator," he said dryly. "In fact, I have two. There's one in the recreation-room bar."

"Then I accept your kind offer." Julie smiled at him.

"You're welcome." Caleb basked in the warmth of her smile.

"Which grocery store do you want?" he asked once they had merged with the heavy lunch-hour traffic.

"I don't care. A grocery store is a grocery store. They all sell frozen dinners and canned pasta."

"Frozen dinners?" He shot her a horrified look.

"And canned pasta," she repeated.

"I was trying to ignore that abomination. No wonder there's nothing to you if you eat like that."

Nothing to you? Julie weighed his words. Did he mean that she was too small physically to be of any interest to him? Julie knew that lots of men went for women who were overly endowed in the bust department. Was Caleb one of them?

Maybe she could get a clue by finding out what his first wife looked like, Julie considered. Surely he would have married his ideal? Although maybe not. The impression she'd gotten from what he'd said was that he'd married Murna because he'd had a bad case of the hots for her.

Julie felt the muscles in her jaw clench at the very idea of Caleb lusting after some woman. It made her feel...

"We'll go to the grocery store I usually shop at," Caleb's voice broke into her unsettling thoughts.

"You do the grocery shopping?" Julie asked. She'd have thought that his housekeeper would have done that.

"Yes, I find cooking to be very relaxing after a busy day. And a cooked meal is a whole lot more nourishing than canned pasta."

"Oh." Julie digested his words. She would never have guessed that a man like Caleb Tarrington would even know where the kitchen was, let alone how to use it.

She stole a glance at him from beneath her thick lashes. There was a whole lot more to him than first met the eye. Not that what first met the eye wasn't pretty spectacular.

"Here we are," Caleb announced as he pulled into a crowded parking lot.

Julie looked curiously at the market Caleb had chosen. It wasn't one of the chains that she usually went to, but a smaller independent.

Following him into the store, Julie watched with approval as he pulled a grocery cart out of the line with the easy competence of someone who has done it hundreds of times before.

"Do you have a list?" Caleb asked her.

"I told you, frozen dinners and canned pasta. And milk and bread."

Caleb simply shook his head.

Julie quickly found the canned-food aisle, and after helping herself to the canned spaghetti went in search of the frozen-foods section, where she tossed a couple of her favorite dinners into the cart.

"Now that you've paid homage to your microwave," he said, "let's get the makings for a real dinner."

Curious about what he would consider a real dinner, Julie followed him toward the meat counter. Instead of stopping in front of the steaks as she'd expected, he continued past it to the seafood section.

"Should we have broiled salmon with fresh blackberry sauce for dinner or grilled shrimp marinated in lime?" he asked.

Julie swallowed as her mouth started salivating at the very thought of any kind of shrimp. Then her mind caught up with her appetite, and what Caleb had said registered. Was he inviting her to eat dinner with him and Will, or was the *we* he'd referred to just him and Will?

She didn't know, and she could hardly ask. If he hadn't meant to include her, she'd sound as if she was finagling an invitation. She stifled a sigh. She hadn't felt this socially inept since she'd been a teenager.

"That shrimp looks pretty fresh," she cautiously offered.

"Shrimp it is," he agreed, leaving her unspoken

question unanswered. He sorted through several bags of fresh shrimp looking for just the right one. "And I think we'll have a mushroom spinach salad with it."

"That sounds..." She paused as something suddenly occurred to her.

"Don't like the idea?" he asked, studying her intent features.

"No," Julie said slowly. "I was just thinking. Cooking involves measuring. And, if you make multiple batches, it involves adding."

"Or dividing, if you make half batches, but what has that got to do with anything?"

"Will needs to work on his math."

"Ah," Caleb said. "The light dawns. We sneak his math lesson in through the back door so to speak."

"So to speak," she agreed. "But we can't cook just anything. We need to choose something that'll capture his interest. Something that tastes good, like cookies. Chocolate-chip cookies."

"Chocolate-chunk cookies," Caleb corrected her. "Chunks make a much better cookie."

"A chip is a chip,"

"Precisely! And a chunk is a chunk. We will have chunks. Come on, let's find the baking aisle." He turned the cart and started to her left.

Julie followed, wondering if chocolate chips really came in chunks or if it was a joke she hadn't quite gotten yet.

To her surprise, she discovered that not only did they make chocolate chunks, but they made them in both milk and semisweet chocolate.

Caleb threw in two bags of chunks, thought a moment, and then added a third.

"Do you like pecans or walnuts in your cookies?" he asked her.

"Pecans," she said, and watched as he tossed in a two-pound sack of pecan halves.

"We'll have the cookies for dessert tonight. You do like chocolate-chunk cookies, don't you?"

"Love 'em," Julie said, feeling her spirits soar. He really had meant to include her in his dinner plans. Suddenly the day seemed brighter than it had just moments before.

Chapter Five

Caleb pulled up in front of the three-car garage behind his house and cut the engine. He shot an apprehensive look at the house, half expecting either his son or his housekeeper to appear with a complaint. It didn't happen. The house sat quietly drowsing in the warm summer sun.

Getting out of the car, he reached into the back seat and handed Julie the blue gym bag with her casual clothes that she had brought with her to the office.

Picking up her sack of food, he said, "We'll put your stuff in the refrigerator and then change into something more comfortable."

"Don't forget to leave out the nuts and the chips for the cookie-making," she reminded him as she followed him along the sidewalk to the kitchen entrance.

"Not chips, chunks," he corrected her. "Chocolate chunks."

Julie grinned at him, feeling incredibly lighthearted

at the thought of the afternoon that stretched before her.

"Once you get them chewed up, it's hardly going to matter," she said.

"That's a form versus function argument, and I'm not buying it," he said.

"No, it isn't. It's a common-sense versus perfectionist argument."

"I am not a perfectionist," Caleb defended himself. "I simply like to do things right the first time. I—"

He broke off as the kitchen door was suddenly pushed open to reveal the housekeeper.

Caleb stiffened at her glum face, bracing himself for bad news. So far, Miss Vincent and Will's disagreements hadn't broken into outright hostilities, but he had the constant feeling that it could happen at any second.

Caleb glanced behind Miss Vincent looking for Will, but the kitchen was empty. A good omen or a bad one? he wondered.

"Good afternoon, Miss Vincent," Caleb offered cautiously.

"We had a very good morning, sir," Miss Vincent responded to the unspoken question in Caleb's voice.

Julie hastily swallowed, turning her inadvertent giggle at Miss Vincent's choice of words into a strangled cough.

Miss Vincent glanced at Julie and then gave her a tentative smile as if unsure how to treat her.

"Hi, Miss Vincent," Julie said cheerfully, trying to reinforce the faint glimmer of friendliness. Miss Vincent could be a powerful ally in teaching Will.

"Miss." Miss Vincent nodded and then turned to

Caleb. "Now that you're here, sir," she said. "I'll leave. My sister and I are going shopping this afternoon."

"Enjoy yourself," Caleb said.

"Oh, and Will is in his room," Miss Vincent added.

Doing what? Julie wondered, but didn't ask. Miss Vincent seemed to be extremely uneasy in her dealings with Will, and Julie didn't want to say anything that might give the woman the feeling that she was being criticized. It was going to be hard enough for Miss Vincent to learn to deal with a lively six-year-old when, according to Caleb, she knew nothing about children, without Julie making her feel defensive.

"Thank you for your help," Caleb said to the housekeeper.

With a perfunctory nod that seemed to be evenly divided between Caleb and Julie, Miss Vincent hastily scooted around them and headed toward the dark-green compact car parked to one side of the driveway.

Julie watched as Miss Vincent climbed into the car. The woman's last furtive look at the house as she backed out of the driveway tugged at Julie's soft heart. Poor thing. She'd had a job with Caleb that she'd obviously liked, and it had all been turned upside down on her through no fault of her own. Life could be very unsettling at times.

"What was so funny?" Caleb asked as he ushered her into the house.

"What do you mean?" Julie shifted her gym bag from one hand to another as she watched him deftly stash her groceries in the refrigerator.

"When Miss Vincent first opened the door, you

looked as if you were struggling not to burst into laughter.''

Julie felt a flicker of unease at his perceptive reading of her reaction.

"It was just how she greeted you,'' Julie tried to explain. "With the announcement that they had had a quiet morning. It reminded me of that old standby in medical movies where the nurse earnestly assures the family that the patient had a good night.''

Caleb grimaced. "There are times lately when I feel like I'm in the middle of a movie. *One Flew Over the Cuckoo's Nest* comes to mind. Or better yet, *Apocalypse Now*.''

"All parents feel that way occasionally.'' Julie used the truth to try to comfort him. "Give it a little time. You and Will hardly know each other.''

Caleb sighed. "I know. Unfortunately, from what Will says, what little he does know about me, he doesn't like.''

"Parenthood is not a popularity contest,'' Julie assured him. "A parent's job is to civilize a child so he can be safely turned loose on the rest of society.''

"Now there's a scary thought! Will versus the real world,'' he said dryly as he tossed the chocolate chunks and the pecans on the counter and then neatly folded the brown paper bag before sticking it under the sink.

"Give it time,'' she said, knowing just how hollow the words must sound to Caleb.

"You really believe I can pull this off?'' he asked slowly.

"I really believe it.'' Julie tried to put every ounce of conviction she could in her words. "Relationships take time to build. Even father-son relationships. You need time to develop common memories and shared experiences.''

''I guess, but I still wish—''

He broke off as Will came running into the room, skidding to a stop when he caught sight of Julie.

''You came back,'' Will said, sounding surprised.

''I said I would,'' Julie reminded him, and then winced when Will's skeptical expression told her far more clearly than anything he could have said just how much faith he put in adults keeping their word.

''I did, too,'' Caleb said.

''You live here. 'Course you came back.'' Will dismissed him.

''What's you gonna do today?'' Will demanded of Julie.

''First, I'm going to change my clothes, and then I think we'll make some cookies,'' Julie said.

Will blinked as if considering the idea and finally asked, ''Why? He—'' Will jabbed a grubby forefinger in Caleb's direction ''—gots him a housekeeper. Housekeepers is supposed t'cook.''

''You should know how to cook so you can be self-sufficient,'' Caleb said. ''What would you do for food if you didn't have a housekeeper?''

''Go to the drive-thru,'' Will said promptly.

''Yes, but—'' Caleb began,

''We are going to make chocolate-chip cookies,'' Julie broke into the pointless argument. One thing Caleb was going to have to learn was that, given half a chance, the average kid could totally tie any parent up in knots with hypothetical arguments. And Will appeared to be far from average.

''Chocolate-chunk,'' Caleb corrected her under his breath.

Julie ignored the correction. "And then after we
have made the cookies, we will clean up the mess,
and then we will eat them."

"I don't like to clean up," Will said,

Julie smiled sympathetically at him. "Actually, I'm
not that keen on it either, Will. But it has to be done
and, since we're going to make the mess, we should
be the ones to clean it up."

"I guess so," Will grumbled, not sounding too
convinced.

"I know so," Julie said cheerfully. "Now then,
show me where I can change my clothes."

"This way," Caleb headed toward the wide mahogany staircase in the front of the house.

"I want to change into something more comfortable, too," he said. "You can use one of the guest
bedrooms."

"Thank you." Julie trotted up the stairs beside
him.

"Hurry up," Will called up after them. "I wants
to eat somma them chocolate-chip cookies."

"Chocolate-chunk," Caleb muttered, and Julie
chuckled.

"You sound like a Greek chorus."

"Weren't all those old Greek plays tragedies?" he
asked.

"Now you're starting to think negatively."

"My life seems to be organized along those lines
recently." Caleb stopped in front of the second door
on the right and pushed it open. "You can use this
room. I'll wait for you."

"Thanks." Julie stepped inside and closed the door
behind her. Her eyebrows lifted in surprise as she
surveyed the room. Like all the rooms she'd seen in

Caleb's house this one was large. But it was also very inviting. A queen-size, mahogany four-poster bed was covered with a fluffy pale-pink silk comforter. Against the headboard, a mound of various-size pillows were stacked, inviting one to snuggle up. A delicate pink-and-green wildflower print decorated the cream wallpaper, and matching drapes outlined the two oversize windows. Through the open door to her right, Julie could see a private bath.

Remembering that Caleb would be waiting, she broke off her inspection of the room and hurriedly upended her gym bag on the bed. Quickly, she slipped out of her business suit and pulled on her jeans and a bright red T-shirt. The walk-in closet provided hangers for her suit.

She spared a second to check her appearance in the dresser's triple mirror and sighed at the image that stared back. She looked like someone's teenage sister. It just wasn't fair! Even if her mother was right, and one day she would be glad to look much younger than she actually was, it didn't help her right now. Now she wanted to look like the competent professional she was.

"You might as well wish to be beautiful and loaded with the kind of sex appeal that sends men into a frenzy, while you're at it," she muttered to herself. A reluctant smile curved her lips at the improbable thought of being followed down the street by men all begging her to accept a date.

Turning away, she opened the bedroom door to find Caleb leaning up against the wall across from her.

Appreciatively, her eyes skimmed over his softly worn jeans and his pale-yellow polo shirt. He looked like a walking advertisement for *Gentleman's Quarterly*.

"Prompt, too," he said.

"Most teachers are," Julie said when what she really wanted to do was ask him what he meant by *too*. But she didn't for fear she might not like the answer.

"A baking we will go, a baking we will go," Julie sang as she came down the staircase beside Caleb.

Caleb smiled at the lilting sound of her singing. The happiness in her voice warmed him. He wanted to gather her close and kiss the sound from her lips. He wanted to absorb some of her abundant joy into his own life.

"You sound funny, lady," Will complained.

"Call me Julie," she reminded him. "And what do you mean, I sound funny?"

"You sound...just wrong." Will struggled to explain. "That song ain't right."

"How should it go?" Julie asked, and Will responded by singing the words in a clear soprano.

Julie chuckled. "Now I understand. You mean I can't carry a tune."

"Not sure," Will muttered. "Just know it ain't right."

"He probably takes after his great-grandmother Frobisher," Caleb said. "She had perfect pitch and never let the rest of the family forget it, either."

"I plead guilty. I can't carry a tune in a bucket. But I refuse to let that stop me. Now then," Julie paused just inside the kitchen and inspected it with an eye toward three people baking in it. There was plenty of space. The restaurant-size stainless-steel refrigerator was directly across from her, and a large commercial stove was to her right. The large center island contained a spare oven as well as twin dish-washers and a second sink.

"Don't like it?" Caleb asked, unable to read the expression on her face as she studied the room.

"Like doesn't begin to describe my feelings. Covet comes a lot closer. This is fantastic. Absolutely perfect. Did you design it yourself?"

A warm feeling flooded Caleb at her unstinting praise.

"Yes," he said. "I wanted something functional with all the latest gadgets, but still looking as if it belonged in a private home."

"You've certainly succeeded," Julie said.

"Are we gonna make them cookies?" Will, tired of being ignored, broke in.

"Yes, and the first step is for you to wash your hands," Julie pointed to the sink.

"Why do I gotta wash 'em?" Will held up his hands and studied his fingers as if surprised to find them still attached.

"To get rid of germs."

"That's dumb! Everybody knows heat kills germs, and we's gonna put them cookies in the oven and cook 'em."

"It's your rebuttal." Caleb grinned at Julie.

"Sorry to disappoint you, kiddo, but washing your hands is not open to discussion. We will observe common-sense health habits, and the most basic one is washing one's hands. I'll go first and then you and then your father."

Julie fitted her words to action and motioned to Will as she dried her hands.

To her relief, Will responded by washing his hands. She really preferred not to get into a power struggle with him at the moment, but it was essential that he learn to follow instructions.

"Will, you go get a pencil and paper while your father gets out the ingredients we'll need."

"Why?" Will asked curiously.

"Because we are going to double the recipe, and we need to write it down so we don't have to keep all that information in our heads."

"Oh. Okay. I gots lots of things in my head. I'm not sure I gots room for lots a 'gredients, too."

Turning, Will raced out of the kitchen.

Caleb surreptitiously watched Julie as he pulled the things they needed to make the cookies out of the cabinets. For someone who looked like an insubstantial fairy, she was one of the most forceful women he'd ever met. Although maybe *forceful* wasn't quite the right word. He studied the soft line of her mouth. She didn't demand, and she didn't intimidate, and she certainly didn't yell. But despite her calm approach, she got exactly what she wanted. And she got it with a minimum of fuss. And without the people around her feeling that she had run roughshod over them.

Maybe it was a skill they taught teachers. And then again...

His eyes lingered on Julie's petite face, maybe it was a gift you were born with.

Julie glanced up to find Caleb staring at her. She shivered slightly at the intensity of his gaze. As if he was trying to read her mind. Or as if his mind was elsewhere and he wasn't really seeing her at all, the more probable explanation occurred to her, and she stifled a sigh. That was undoubtedly it. Men never saw her. Never really saw her. She was simply there. And the men she knew were pretty unremarkable. Nowhere near as compulsively appealing as Caleb Tarrington. If they didn't think she was worthy of a second look, Caleb Tarrington certainly wasn't going to consider her.

"I gots a pen and paper!" Will's shout preceded him into the room. "Now what?"

"Now we double the recipe." Julie took one of the sacks of chocolate chunks and sat down at the kitchen table. "Come help."

Will obediently came, slipping into the chair beside her.

Caleb watched as Julie bent toward Will. Her whole body posture was one of caring. Of protection. What would Will have been like if he had married someone like Julie in the first place? he wondered. What would his own life have been like?

He clenched his teeth in rejection of the tantalizing images that sprang to mind. Speculation was pointless.

The cookie-making went better than Julie had expected. Not that she'd expected much, but Will had been fascinated by the process from start to finish.

"Can I take somma these cookies out onto the patio and eat 'em?" Will demanded the moment he'd finished stacking the dirty bowls on the counter and had thrown out the trash.

"Sure, just a second, and I'll put them on a plate for you," Julie said. "How about a glass of milk to go with them?"

"No! Do you know where milk comes from?" Will demanded.

Julie glanced over at Caleb who was carefully transferring hot cookies to the cooling rack. He shook his head as if disclaiming any knowledge of what Will was talking about.

"Despite the fact that I feel like a straight man, I'll ask anyway," Julie said. "Where does milk come from?"

"Cows!" An expression of disgust wrinkled Will's small face. "The insida cows."

Julie pursed her lips as she tried to think of something to say. She couldn't.

"It's true," Will insisted at her continued silence. "I know 'cause Mom had this friend who had a ranch, and we went to visit him, and he showed me how they milk cows. It was yucky! I ain't drinking nothing what comes from the insida no cow!"

Will took the plate of cookies she handed him and headed for the patio, still grumbling about the horrors of milk.

Caleb chuckled at the expression on Julie's face. "What now, child expert?"

His teasing voice did odd things to her sense of equilibrium. For an instant she felt close to him. Almost as if Will was theirs. As if their relationship was much closer than that of teacher and parent. She ignored her reaction in favor of answering Caleb's question.

"For starters, I'd call his pediatrician and ask about calcium substitutes. But you know…" Julie's voice trailed away.

"I know lots of things. Which particular thing are your referring to?" Laughter threaded Caleb's voice.

"When you think about it, getting milk from cows is kind of gross."

"Don't think about it," he said.

Telling someone not to think about something

never worked, Julie thought. If it did, she'd have been able to banish Caleb from her thoughts.

"You're probably right," she finally said. "And he'll probably outgrow his aversion to milk. In the meantime, let's get the kitchen cleaned up. Do you want to load the dishwasher or wipe off the counters?"

"What?" Caleb stared at her in surprise. She was actually intending to help with the mess?

Julie blinked at his incredulous expression.

"I'd said I'd help clean up. Between the two of us, we can be done in ten minutes."

"I know you said you would, but..."

He broke off. He could hardly tell her that his first wife had always said she'd help, too, and she never had. She had simply walked away from the messes she'd created, leaving others to clean up after her. Much as she had walked away from the mess she'd made of raising their son and left it to him to try to put it right.

"I'll load the dishwasher," he finally said. "You can wipe off the counters."

"Right." She gave him a cheerful smile and turned to the sink.

Caleb absently loaded the dishwasher, his total attention on Julie as she cleaned the countertops. Her slender hands moved competently over the granite in rhythmic sweeps.

Sharing this simple, homey task with Julie gave Caleb an odd feeling. A feeling of... He studied the sway of her enticing body as she worked, trying to pin down the sensation. It wasn't exactly sexual, although she was certainly sexually appealing.

No, it was a lot more than just a desire to grab her and kiss her senseless. It was a feeling of...

Companionship. That was it. He finally was able to identify the elusive emotion. Cleaning up the kitchen with Julie gave him a sense of companionship. Of belonging. Of being part of a family. Something that had been missing from his life since he was a young man, when his parents had still been alive. And even though he knew that his feeling wasn't real, it was still a very appealing fantasy. One that tugged at something deep inside him. He hadn't even been aware it was there until he'd met Julie Raffet.

"There." She took a final swipe at the countertop and then draped the wet dishcloth over the edge of the sink. "All clean."

Caleb studied her small delicate features, and an irrepressible sense of devilment gripped him. "Not quite all clean," he corrected.

Julie swept a quick glance over the now-sparkling countertops and looked back at him questioningly. Her breath caught in her throat as he walked closer, stopping scant inches from her. Her eyes widened as contradictory emotions tore through her. One part of her wanted to retreat from his almost aggressive masculinity, while another part of her wanted to move closer to him. To bask in that same masculinity. To revel in just how different they really were.

"I think I got it all," she said brightly, mentally wincing at the breathless sound of her voice. She sounded like a teenager who'd suddenly been addressed by the captain of the football team. Not like the mature woman she knew herself to be.

"I wasn't talking about the counters," he said. "I

was talking about you. You put yourself heart and soul into your cooking.

"Face, too." His voice lowered seductively, and Julie held her breath as she watched his hand come closer. His fingertips touched her cheekbone and trailed down her cheek. The friction of his gently moving fingers sent sparks zinging over her skin, tightening it.

"You've got flour on you..." the hypnotic sound of his voice held her captive to his exploring fingertips. "Here." He lightly brushed her cheek.

Julie gulped, trying to think of a breezy comeback, but she couldn't drag a single rational thought out of the maelstrom of emotions swirling through her. All she could do was wait. Wait and see what he would do next.

"And right here..." he continued. His tone sounded almost absent to Julie. As if his mind was elsewhere. "There is most definitely a bit of chocolate."

He leaned closer, and Julie stopped thinking altogether and simply felt. Felt the intoxicating sensation of his lips as they touched the side of her mouth.

She jumped as the tip of his tongue touched the edge of her mouth. As if he was tasting the bit of chocolate he'd pointed out. It was the most incredibly erotic sensation she'd ever felt, and it was the hardest thing she'd ever done not to throw herself in his arms and beg him to kiss her properly.

A devastating sense of loss filled her when he raised his head and stepped back.

Why had he done that? The muddled question ricocheted through her mind. She stared at the smooth tanned column of his neck, trying desperately to think. Trying to push her emotions into the background and think instead of feel. It was hard. Very hard. Feeling was much more rewarding than thinking. Thinking was sterile and cold and only served to remind her of the inherent dangers of what she was feeling.

Nonetheless, she persisted. Why had Caleb stopped short of a real kiss? For that matter, why had he touched her in the first place. His caress had almost seemed...indulgent, she finally decided.

She might have found it incredibly appealing, but he'd undoubtedly been indulging in a bit of masculine teasing. It wouldn't have meant anything to a sophisticated man like Caleb Tarrington. The thought steadied her as nothing else.

It was imperative that he not realize just how affected she had been. And the only way she could think to accomplish that was for her to continue to treat him exactly as she had before. As a casual friend.

Taking a deep breath, she said, ''I tend to put my whole self into what I do.''

''So I see,'' Caleb murmured.

''And now I'd better continue with Will's math lesson.'' She relaxed a bit at the even sound of her voice. He wouldn't be able to tell just how profoundly his caress had shaken her from her voice. Her odd susceptibility to him was still her secret.

Julie gave him what she hoped was her normal smile and went out to the patio to find Will.

Caleb watched her go, prey to a confusing mixture of emotions. Annoyance at himself for so quickly forgetting his intention of treating her as off limits; fear that she might be annoyed at him; and chagrin that his caress hadn't even shaken her composure, while his own blood pressure was so jacked up he could hear his heart pounding in his ears. He wanted to run after her, grab her and kiss her until she was as shaken as he was. Until she couldn't think about anyone else, even his own son.

He shook his head as if to dislodge the impulse. What was the matter with him? he wondered uneasily. Surely he didn't begrudge his own son Julie's undivided attention?

He went into the recreation room and stared out through the open French doors at the patio where Julie was bent toward Will, obviously explaining something to him. Caleb sank into the down-filled sofa and studied them, trying to sort through his turbulent emotions.

He didn't begrudge his son Julie's attention, he finally decided. On the contrary. Seeing Julie focus on Will made him feel complete. It reinforced his initial feeling that they were a unit, which in a very limited way, they were. Will was the student, Julie was the teacher, and he was...

What exactly was his role in their relationship? Did he even have a role in Julie's mind? he wondered. He knew she'd only agreed to help him for Will's sake. That had been only too clear. He didn't even seem to register with her as a man. She treated him with the casualness of someone she'd known all her life. And had never been impressed with. The thought rankled.

Even knowing that he was being childish didn't entirely banish the feeling. On some level, he craved Julie's acknowledgment of him as...as a what? What exactly did he want her to see him as?

He wasn't sure. And that very uncertainty, when

he was normally so certain about all areas of his life, made him very uneasy.

As he watched, Will said something that made Julie's incredible smile flash across her face. She really was a good teacher.

But then he already knew that, he reminded himself. That's why he'd gone to see her in the first place. Because she was a dedicated career woman. Like his first wife. The chilling thought made him shift uneasily on the sofa.

The sound of Will's shout about something distracted him, and he got to his feet. Outside with the pair of them was where he wanted to be. Not sitting in here by himself. He'd already spent far too much of his life alone.

Chapter Six

"Julie, there're a couple of things in the morning mail that need to be taken care of immediately."

Julie abandoned the notes she was transcribing into the computer in favor of watching Caleb's graceful stride as he walked toward her. His suit jacket had disappeared somewhere, and he'd rolled up the sleeves of his immaculate white shirt. His navy-and-green striped tie had been tugged loose to allow him to unbutton the top button on his shirt. He looked exactly like what he was, a very busy, very successful executive who was already deeply emerged in the day's work despite it barely being nine o'clock.

He also looked like a walking advertisement for virile masculinity, Julie thought. So much so that she was finding it increasingly difficult to remember her role as his secretary. Her feminine side kept insisting on thinking of far more interesting things than business.

"I've jotted down some notes on these letters," Caleb said.

Julie blinked, struggling to focus her attention on his words and not the fascinating timbre of the voice uttering them. It was hard. She so much preferred to simply look at his fascinating body. To daydream about what she'd like to do with it.

Grow up, Julie! she told herself, and then almost giggled at the incongruity of the order. The problem was that she was grown-up. Grown-up enough to appreciate and be intrigued by the most gorgeous specimen of masculinity she'd ever come in contact with.

Caleb watched the flicker of humor that momentarily lit her eyes, wondering what she found amusing. It couldn't be his comment about the correspondence.

Her unexpected flash of humor probably had nothing to do with him, he told himself. Simply because he couldn't get her out of his mind didn't mean that she gave him a single thought from one day to the next.

Walking around the desk, he set the papers he was carrying on top of the data she had been entering in the computer.

"The top letter needs to be dealt with first," he began.

Julie tensed as Caleb leaned forward, and his physical presence engulfed her, rattling her composure. She took a deep steadying breath and peered down at the letter he'd referred to.

Edwards University, Julie read the letterhead at the top of the page. What did a university...

Her train of thought was derailed when Caleb tapped his forefinger on the note he'd scrawled in the margin, and she was mesmerized by the movement.

"Tell them that the Tarrington Foundation will pay the young man's tuition as well as give him a stipend for fees and books, but that I would suggest that he consider cutting back on the number of classes he plans to take each semester. I'm still willing to foot the bill even if he isn't a full-time student. It'll take him a year longer, but he's less likely to collapse under the strain of the killing schedule he's set for himself."

"Who is he?" Julie asked curiously, remembering what her sister had said about Caleb quietly supporting quite a few charities.

"A very promising kid, who had a full-time scholarship from a private company, but when his father died unexpectedly last year, he had to drop out of college to help his mother and younger sisters. Once he did that, he lost his scholarship, and now he can't afford to return to school without substantial financial help."

"And you're going to give it to him," Julie said, her eyes widening as she read the second paragraph and realized just how much money Caleb was investing in this young man.

"I'm giving him a hand *up,* not a hand out," Caleb said. "Considering what the poor kid's already been through, he deserves help.

"Now, about the second letter." Caleb determinedly changed the subject as if embarrassed by his own generosity. "Tell that group of smugly self-satisfied jerks I have no intention of speaking at their pompous dinner."

"Your scheduling precludes your acceptance of their flattering request," Julie paraphrased.

"To say nothing of my common sense, they—" Caleb broke off as the phone rang.

Julie picked up the receiver and answered with a crisp, "Tarrington and Associates. May I help you?"

It immediately became obvious to Caleb that the call was not business-related. At least, not to his business.

"Yes, sir," Julie said. "No, of course this isn't a bad time to talk."

Caleb frowned in disagreement. It most emphatically was a bad time for her to talk. He was trying to explain something important to her. Something about business, and this was an office the last time he checked.

His sense of ill usage deepened as he listened to Julie's enthusiastic voice talking about phonics. Why was she describing a method of teaching word sounds to someone on the phone?

As if in answer to his unspoken question, Julie covered the mouthpiece of the phone and whispered, "It's the chairman of the hiring committee at the charter school I interviewed at."

Caleb could feel the muscles of his jaw clench in annoyance at her explanation. So that was why she sounded so enthused. Because the phone call was about furthering her career.

But he already knew her primary focus was her career, he reminded himself, trying to be fair. Julie Raffet was a woman to whom teaching would always take center stage in her life.

"Sorry about that," she said perfunctorily as she hung up, "But one of the members of the hiring committee had a follow-up question about my teaching methods."

"And did they like your answer?" he asked, curious in spite of his irritation at the interruption.

Julie shrugged. "Who knows. There's always a certain amount of politics involved in hiring teachers. Sometimes a member of the hiring committee will have a favorite candidate and try to get rid of the competition."

Caleb's dark eyebrows rose in surprise. "Politics in grade-school hiring?"

"Anytime two people get together to do anything, there are politics involved," she said dryly.

"But what about getting the best teachers for the kids?" Caleb felt a sense of outrage that anyone could spend five minutes with Julie and not see that she was a dedicated teacher who put the children's interests above her own.

"The theory is that all certified teachers are equally competent to teach."

Caleb snorted. "No one can be dumb enough to believe that."

Julie gave a delicate sniff. "You'd be surprised just how dumb people can be when they're protecting their turf. Or maybe you wouldn't be. I imagine it's pretty much the same in every profession."

"To a certain extent," Caleb agreed. "But when you run your own company, you don't have to worry about it so much. Maybe you ought to open your own school."

She shuddered. "Heaven forbid!"

"Why not?" Caleb asked curiously. John was only the second person he'd known who'd gone into education, and John had had his sights set on being a superintendent of a large metropolitan school from day one of his teaching career.

"Because I can think of nothing I'd hate more than having to spend my days handling administrative stuff. Dealing with paperwork and scheduling problems is boring," she said succinctly. "The classroom is where things happen. That's where you can make a difference. Where you can actually change a kid's life. Where…"

The ringing phone broke into her impassioned words.

Julie automatically answered it as if she'd been doing it for years.

"Oh, hi, Joe," she said, "What do you want?"

Caleb bit back the urge to say something very rude. He didn't know what this Joe wanted, but he sure knew what he'd like. Five uninterrupted minutes of Julie's time so they could get some work done.

Caleb listened with growing impatience as Julie laughed at something her caller said. He didn't want her laughing with another man. At least, not during working hours. He tried to justify his reaction. He wanted her to focus on what needed to be done, not…

Joe? Caleb frowned as he suddenly placed the name. A man named Joe had left a message on Julie's phone answering machine the other day. Was this the same Joe? The phone message had sounded as if they knew each other very well. As did the conversation they were having now. An unexpected flash of jealousy shot through him.

Caleb made a valiant effort to squash it, knowing that jealousy was not only small-minded but also irrational. Especially in this case. He had no reason to be jealous of Julie, because there was nothing between them. She didn't mean anything to him personally. She was simply his son's tutor. That was all, he assured himself. And the fact that he was constantly fantasizing about her was nothing more than the fact that he was a normal, healthy man, and she was a gorgeous, fascinating woman.

He scowled as she laughed again, and his jumbled emotions tipped over into outrage.

"When you finally remember that this is an office, not a social club, I'll be in my office!" Caleb snapped.

He stalked back into his office, seething anger evident in the rigid set of his back.

Julie blinked, caught completely off guard by his outburst. What on earth... She winced as Caleb closed the door to his office with a decided snap.

"Listen, Joe, I've got to cut this short. The other line is ringing," she made an excuse. "Just try flowers and a small, intimate restaurant. Bye."

Julie slowly replaced the phone, her eyes never leaving Caleb's closed door. The very oak it was made of seemed to radiate disapproval.

While she was willing to admit that he was right in saying this was a business, it was also true that theirs was hardly a normal business relationship. She was only here as a favor to Caleb. She was not an employee in the normal sense of the word. And that being so, he should be only too happy to cut her some slack. So why wasn't he? she wondered.

She didn't know, but she had no intention of letting this pass. It had to be discussed. She would explain the situation to him from her point of view and tell him either to give her some leeway to take care of personal business or to give her a very good reason why he wouldn't.

The sooner this was settled the better.

Determinedly getting to her feet, she reached down for the letters he'd left behind and headed toward his office. Small misunderstandings, which were left to fester, invariably became bigger misunderstandings, and she didn't want that to happen. She enjoyed Caleb's company too much to risk anything that might damage their relationship.

Julie gave a perfunctory knock on Caleb's office door and then pushed it open.

Caleb looked up from his desk and snapped, "Are your personal calls over?"

"For the moment. I came to get the rest of your input on the letters."

"Are you sure you can spare the time!" he snipped, listening to his own words, which seemed to hang in the air between them with stunned disbelief. What was the matter with him? he wondered in dismay. He sounded like a surly teenager instead of the mature, responsible adult that he was.

"I can spare the time for your letters," she said calmly, refusing to be drawn into his anger. "And while I'm doing that, why don't you take the time to examine your response to my phone calls?"

"This is a business," he began, seemingly unable to back down now that he'd started.

"Quite true," she agreed. "And while I can understand your frustration at having your work interrupted, I really think it is not unreasonable of me to expect you to cut me a little slack. I'm not a regular employee. I am merely substituting until Miss Andrews can return. And I'm doing it on very short notice. I haven't had time to totally rearrange my schedule."

"So I'm supposed to rearrange mine!"

"Waiting a few minutes for me to take two phone calls hardly constitutes a major rearrangement of anything."

Caleb stared at Julie's serene features, fighting to get a grip on his seething emotions. How could she be so calm when he felt as if someone had dumped every emotion he was capable of feeling into a blender and switched it on high?

Because her own emotions weren't involved, the obvious answer occurred to him. Not only that, but their argument wasn't following the pattern he was used to. In every single argument he'd ever had with Murna, she had immediately launched into a very personal, very vicious attack on his basic worth as a person. Julie hadn't done that. Every word she had said had been about the point of their conflict. Nothing had been directed at him personally. And she had a right to hurl a few charges at him too, he conceded. He was behaving like an absolute jerk.

"Well?" Julie watched the emotions flitting across his face, wondering what he was thinking. "Are you going to try to be a little more reasonable?"

Caleb got to his feet and started toward her. "You're absolutely right," he said.

Julie blinked under the force of the intriguing smile that so unexpectedly curved his mouth. He looked incredibly attractive. He also looked like a man who was up to something. Something that had nothing to do with phone calls.

A flutter of excitement scattered her thoughts as he came closer still.

"I have been exceedingly unreasonable." Caleb clearly enunciated the words as he closed the distance between them.

Julie swallowed uneasily as he stopped scant inches from her. The sheer force of his physical presence seemed to crowd her. Making her feel on edge.

She raised her gaze from the closely shaven skin of his chin to find her eyes caught by the emotion swirling through his bright blue eyes. But what kind of emotion was the million-dollar question, and she didn't have a clue. His nearness was making a mockery of her normal thought processes. It was all she could do to hold her ground, let alone analyze anything.

Her breath caught in her throat as he leaned forward slightly, towering over her. Julie could feel the heat from his large body engulf her, tightening her muscles. Making her aware of him in a way she had never before been aware of a man. She felt quintessentially feminine and emotionally vulnerable, but the odd thing was she didn't feel threatened. On the contrary, she felt...invigorated.

"And now that I've apologized for my boorish behavior, I think we ought to kiss and make up," Caleb announced.

"Kiss and make up?" Julie repeated uncertainly, scrambling to make sense of this latest development. One minute he'd been all bent out of shape because she was getting personal phone calls and the next, he seemed to be a teasing man intent on playing sexual games with her. She just wished she knew the rules to the game because, much as she wanted to play, she had a nasty feeling there was no way for her to win.

But on the other hand, if she knew going in that this was a no-win situation, it should be all right. Because she didn't need to win, she rationalized. She just didn't want to lose. And there was a lot of ground in between the two extremes.

He slowly lowered his head as if giving her time to object, and when she didn't, he slipped his arms around her slight body and gathered her closer. His lips touched hers with the faintest of pressure.

Fiancée, the single word surfaced through the pleasure flooding him. He was supposed to be treating Julie like his best friend's fiancée, he belatedly remembered. He struggled gamely to force himself to end the kiss, but it became impossible when she trembled. Instinctively, he deepened the pressure, and her lips parted.

He'd get a new best friend, he thought foggily.

Caleb tasted of coffee and ever so faintly of something else. Something more elusive and infinitely more appealing. Julie tried to catalog what she was feeling in an attempt to slow down her headstrong response. It was impossible. Sensation piled upon sensation and all she could do was feel.

Finally, she gave up the impossible effort and surrendered to his kiss, reveling in what this man made her feel.

Long before she was ready to quit, Caleb raised his head and stared down into her bemused face for a long moment. Dropping a final kiss on the tip of her small nose, he said, "Friends again?"

Julie stared blankly at him, struggling to escape the sensual trap in which she was so firmly immersed.

"Friends," Julie forced the word out past the tight muscles in her throat, struggling to match his level of sophistication.

"Good." Caleb took the letters out of her limp hand and moved back. "Now, about this third letter.

It's to a contractor who is so far behind schedule, he's throwing the whole project off.''

Julie followed Caleb as he returned to his desk as if drawn by an invisible string. How could he so easily throw off the effects of their kiss? she wondered in confusion. The only logical answer was that Caleb hadn't found it as unsettling as she had. But it didn't matter how unsettling she found his kisses, Julie tried to reassure herself. As long as Caleb didn't realize it. The thought stiffened her pride, enabling her to listen to him tell her with apparent serenity, what he wanted her to write to the contractor.

Hoping that she'd understood enough to be able to write a coherent letter to the recalcitrant contractor, Julie retreated to the relative safety of her office the moment she could.

Caleb watched the door close behind her with a twofold sense of disappointment. First, that she had closed the door, and he could no longer simply look out and see her working at her desk, and second, that she seemed so unaffected by his kiss, when he had been so…

He ran his fingers through his dark hair in frustration as he tried to figure out what was happening to him. He'd kissed women before. Kissed quite a few of them, in fact. But not one of the women he'd ever kissed had even come close to affecting him the way kissing Julie Raffet had.

But why? He began to pace across his office, too agitated to sit still. What was it about Julie Raffet that made him forsake his intention of not kissing her the minute he got the chance?

Maybe it was because when she'd kissed him, she'd put her whole self into it. When they'd kissed, he hadn't been left with the feeling that her mind was busily speculating on his financial worth or worrying that he might disturb her makeup. When he'd kissed Julie, he'd had the intoxicating feeling that the only thing that mattered to her at that moment was his kiss. That her whole focus was on him. For that moment in time, he was the only thing in the world that mattered to her.

What would it be like to make love to a woman who gave you her total attention? he wondered, and then had to hastily chop off the tantalizing images that flooded his mind when his body began to react.

Caleb grimaced in self-disgust. This was just great. In a matter of days he had gone from a rational adult male in total control of his life to spending valuable working time mooning over a woman who treated him like a friend. Even worse, like a friend of no particular value.

"Grow up, man," he ordered himself as he determinedly sat back down at his desk. He didn't have the time to indulge in erotic daydreams. He had work to do. Now. He reached for the notes he'd made on the shopping-mall project, determined to get the preliminary plans done before they finished at noon.

Despite his best efforts, Caleb still wasn't done when Julie opened his office door shortly after noon and said, "Time to be off."

"Be with you in a minute," Caleb said as he began to gather up work to take home.

"I sent off all the correspondence." Julie watched him shove folder after folder into his briefcase. Surely he wasn't going to try to do all that tonight, she worried. When was he planning on sleeping?

"That should be enough." He finally stopped. Grabbing his suit jacket, he shrugged into it, picked up his briefcase and headed toward the waiting Julie. Despite the frustrations of the morning, he felt light-hearted. He was going home to his son in the company of a fascinating woman.

"I'm parked to the right," he told her once they had reached the parking lot.

"Me, too."

"You got your car back from the garage?"

"Last night. They replaced a few wires and some whatsits."

Caleb stopped beside her battered car and eyed it critically. "And now it runs as good as new?"

Julie laughed, and the lighthearted sound bubbled through him. "Actually, I have no idea. Palladin was ten years old before I ever got him."

"I'll follow you home," Caleb said.

"Don't worry, I won't have any problems."

As a prediction, it was a total flop. Three-quarters of the way to Caleb's home, her car sputtered to a stop in the middle of a busy intersection, coughed twice and died.

Julie struggled to restart it as several of the cars in line behind her leaned on their horns.

"Idiots," she muttered to herself in exasperation. "Do they think I'm blocking traffic for the fun of it?"

"They aren't thinking," Caleb's voice came from right outside her open driver's window and instantly soothed her frazzled nerves. She wasn't alone with a dead car. Caleb was here to help her.

"Let me try it." He opened the door.

Julie scooted across the seat to the passenger side as he slid into the driver's seat.

She watched as he turned the key in the ignition, her concentration on his long fingers and not on the grinding sounds coming from the car. Caleb was far more interesting than her car.

"Get that damn car out of the intersection!" someone yelled from behind them.

"Inelegantly expressed, but, nonetheless, sound advice," Caleb said.

Julie got out of the car when Caleb did and watched as he slipped off his suit jacket and tossed it into the back of his car.

"Get back in your car and put it in neutral," Caleb said as he started to roll up his shirtsleeves. "I'll push you to the side of the road."

"You can't push the car yourself," Julie protested. "You'll wind up with a…a hernia!"

"I don't want you out here in traffic," Caleb said flatly. "It's dangerous."

"He's right, miss," a burly man spoke from behind them.

"Sure is," his companion said. "One of these damn fools zipping around you could turn you into a traffic statistic."

"Now, there's a cheery thought," Julie said. "But I still think I ought to help."

"I need someone to steer while I push," Caleb said. "You're the logical choice since you have the least amount of muscle to contribute to the effort."

"Not that what muscle you got isn't nice," the burly man said with heavy-handed gallantry, "but you can help best by steering."

"Right." Julie gave in to their logic. Women might be men's equals in lots of ways, but brute strength wasn't one of them.

With Caleb and the two good Samaritans helping, it only took a few moments to push her car out of the heavy flow of traffic.

Once it was safely parked on the side of the road, Julie grabbed her purse and her gym bag with her casual clothes from the back seat and got out.

"Thank you so much for your help," she told the two men who had helped. "I really appreciate your stopping."

"Our pleasure," the heavyset man said while his companion merely nodded. "Take care now, miss."

"I will, and thanks again."

Julie watched them get back into the delivery truck they had been driving, and then turned back to Caleb who was staring at her.

"Is something wrong?" she asked, taken aback by the intensity of his gaze.

"No." He absently opened his car door for her, his mind still replaying how she had thanked the two men. That was all she had done. Thanked them. There had been no sexual flirtatiousness in her words or her manner. No innuendo. Just a simple, sincere thanks. Not at all like his ex-wife, who had injected sexuality into every contact she had ever had with a man.

Julie waited until he was in the car and safely buckled in and then asked, "Then why are you a million miles... Caleb—" she grabbed his arm as he tried to start his car "—did you pull something? Or strain something?"

The concern in her voice sent a shaft of some unexpected emotion through him. For a second he felt cherished. As if his well-being was really important to her. And in a way it probably was. He came down to earth with a thump. Along with the well-being of fifty or so of her students.

"I'm fine," he said. "I was just thinking that it's time you quit beating a dead horse and get a new car."

"What a disgusting analogy," she said.

"Maybe, but it's accurate." Caleb checked the traffic in his side mirror before he pulled into the road. "We go right past a car dealership on the way home. Why don't we take a quick stop and see what they've got."

"No, thanks. I'll just fix the old one."

"You already tried that. It didn't work."

Julie bit her lip, trying to decide what to say and finally opted for the unvarnished truth. "I can't buy a car because I can't afford it," she said. "I used every penny of my savings as a down payment on my house when I bought it in April. And the two graduate classes I'm taking this summer, I'm paying for by installments. I don't have room in my budget for car payments until next winter. November to be precise."

"I'll buy you a car," Caleb instinctively offered.

"No." Julie flatly refused his offer. At the moment, their relationship was that of equals. If she accepted an expensive gift from him, everything would change. And not for the better.

"But…" Caleb started, and then shut up when he saw her stiff expression. Damn! He had embarrassed her, and he hadn't meant to. All he had wanted to do was to make sure she had safe, reliable transportation. That and secure his own peace of mind. The very thought of her driving around after dark in a car liable to break down at any minute made him feel faintly frantic. But now was not the time to press it. Tonight he'd figure out the best way to convince her to let him buy her a car. In the meantime, she could simply ride with him. The thought cheered him immensely.

Chapter Seven

"That's the mailman's truck I just heard," Will announced.

"And that's your math, kiddo." Julie pointed to the pile of red counters on the patio table that Will was using to try to understand set theory.

"But I have to get the mail!" Will gave her a gaze of wide-eyed innocence. "I think it's a federal law."

Julie chuckled. "Think again."

Will seemed to take her seriously. He twisted his small face into a mask of intense concentration, and then finally said, "Maybe there's a kidnap note in it. Maybe Dad was snatched, and they've sent the ransom note and, if'n we don't go get it now, something awful will happen to him."

Julie arched her light-brown eyebrows. "Kidnapped on his way to the grocery store?"

"And it would all be my fault 'cause I ate all the bread, and he had to go get more and, if'n we don't get the ransom note, I'll be scarred for life!'' Will fixed her with a mournful look.

Julie chuckled. ''If you want a break that badly, go get the mail.

''And don't dawdle,'' she called after him as he raced around the side of the house to the mailbox beside the front door.

Julie smiled as he disappeared. Will had the most active imagination of anyone she had ever met. She just wished it wasn't fueled by the host of totally unsuitable movies he had been allowed to watch.

Within minutes he came tearing back and skidded to a halt in front of her.

''Lookee, Julie. I gots me a package!'' He shoved a flat parcel about the size of a sheet of paper in her face.

Julie pushed it back far enough so that she could read the address.

''You sure do.'' She automatically stacked the letters Will had tossed on the table.

''Who's it from?'' she asked.

''What?''

''Who sent it to you?''

''Oh.'' Will squinted at the return label. ''It's from Mom. I wonder why she sent it.''

''She probably misses you,'' Julie suggested, even though she didn't believe it for a minute. In Julie's opinion, any woman who would ship her own son off to a father the child had never met wasn't about to miss him. But even if she was right, it didn't matter. Will was better off believing his mother loved him.

''Mom?'' He looked up in surprise. ''Nah, she don't miss me. I's a kid, and kids and adults have separate lives.'' Will repeated something he had obviously been told many times.

"What is it?'' Julie asked when Will had finished opening the package.

"It's a picture.'' Will set it down on the table in front of Julie. "Of my mom. See?'' He picked up the enclosed note and read it, "Mom says it's for me to put by my bed.''

"I see,'' Julie said slowly as she looked down at the photo. Staring back up at her was the face of an exquisitely beautiful woman. And she was beautiful, Julie conceded. Not striking or distinguished or well made up, but drop-dead beautiful. No normal woman could ever hope to compete with Murna's looks, Julie realized with a sense of dismay that she refused to examine too closely.

"Does she really look like that?'' Julie couldn't resist the question.

Will sucked on his lower lip as he considered the question. "No,'' he finally said. "Not 'xactly. Here she's smiling, and she don't smile much.''

"Oh,'' Julie muttered, having no idea what to say, so she chose discretion and remained silent.

"Back to your set theory, Will,'' she said.

"Ain't mine,'' he grumbled. "Math is stupid.''

"Then it's fortunate that you aren't,'' Julie said cheerfully.

Still grumbling, Will bent over his counters, and then suddenly jumped to his feet as Caleb pulled into the driveway.

"It's Dad!'' Will yelled.

"Sure is,'' Julie said, feeling the same sense of pleasure at Caleb's return as Will, but for different reasons. She watched approvingly as Caleb shifted his sack of groceries from his right hand to his left and affectionately ruffled Will's silky hair.

"You'll never guess what I discovered." Caleb gave Julie a triumphant grin that zinged through her like the bubbles in a glass of champagne.

She smiled back, finding his good humor irresistible. "What did you find?"

"Calcium-fortified orange juice!" He extracted a brightly colored container and set it on the table in front of her, accidentally scattering Will's counters in all directions.

Julie gave them a cursory glance and then dismissed them as totally unimportant.

"It says," Caleb continued, "that a glass of this contains as much calcium as a glass of milk."

"I likes orange juice," Will said. "It comes from an orange."

"I think I'll take a break from all this boring stuff and drink some," Will said with a cautious look at Julie. "I's worked real hard, and my brain's tired."

Julie chuckled. "It wouldn't be quite so tired if it didn't have to think of so many imaginative excuses. Take the groceries out to the kitchen and put them away, Will. Then you can have a fifteen-minute break."

"I's not sure my brain'll be recovered by then," Will tried.

"If a short break won't help, then maybe Julie shouldn't give you one at all," Caleb said.

"S'okay," Will hastily backtracked. "But the fifteen minutes starts after I gets them groceries put away."

"Definitely the judge's offspring," Caleb muttered as he watched Will race into the house.

Julie smiled at Caleb's rueful expression. "I'm beginning to wish I could have met the judge," she said.

"You'd have liked him. And he would have liked you. He always said that teachers were the backbone of any free society."

"A perceptive man. By the way, the mail came." Julie handed him the letters Will had fetched.

He gave them a perfunctory look and shoved them into the back pocket of his jeans.

"What was this?" He gestured toward the crumpled brown paper that Will had tossed on the table.

"Will got a present from his mother." Julie picked up the picture and handed it to Caleb.

Surreptitiously, Julie watched as Caleb glanced down at it. She couldn't read any reaction in his face. None. He could have been looking at a blank piece of paper instead of at a gorgeous woman to whom he'd once been married. Why? The question nagged at her. Was there no reaction because the sight of his ex-wife meant so little to him? Or was he showing no reaction because he cared so much that he didn't dare let any emotion show?

The possibility bothered Julie even though she knew it shouldn't. Caleb's emotions didn't have anything to do with her. Not even the fact that he'd kissed her changed that. She might not have had a great deal of experience with men, but it didn't take much experience to know that a man could kiss or, for that matter, make love to a woman and not be deeply emotionally involved.

"Is it a good likeness?" Julie probed, even though her common sense told her to leave the whole subject alone.

Caleb frowned slightly as if considering her question and then said, "Yes, it's a very good likeness."

"She's one of the most beautiful women I've ever seen." Julie forced the honest assessment out.

"Definitely, but her beauty is like a deadly flower that lures insects to their death," he said dispassionately.

"What!"

"It may sound harsh, but it's true. Our culture leads us to believe that if a person is beautiful, then they must also possess a host of other virtues. Those fairy tales of yours are a perfect example," Caleb insisted at her skeptical expression.

"The heroine is always portrayed as beautiful. Cinderella, Rose Red, Snow White. So our kids grow up thinking that if a person is beautiful on the outside they must be equally beautiful on the inside."

He grimaced. "I sure as hell did. I took one look at Murna and instantly endowed her with every virtue known to man."

"Well, you were rather young," Julie said, wondering if his words meant that he was off beautiful women altogether or only that he intended to get to know a beautiful woman better before he got involved emotionally with her.

She stifled a sigh of frustration. It seemed that for every bit of personal information she discovered about Caleb, two more questions arose. But at least she now knew one important fact, she consoled herself. Caleb was not still in love with his ex-wife.

Rather young. Julie's assessment echoed through his mind. His failed marriage had always loomed in the back of his mind as a monstrous calamity that would forever warp his life. And yet, Julie's words had made the whole episode sound like nothing more than a youthful mistake he'd outgrown.

Could she be right? Could he have put too much emphasis on his past mistake? Could he have grown beyond it? Grown enough to now be able to make a rational judgment about a woman? A woman like...

"I still gots one minute!" Will came rushing back, breaking into his thought.

Julie stifled a sigh at the interruption and then told herself that she was being ridiculous. She was here to tutor Will, not to talk to his father.

"This stuff's good." Will held up a full glass of juice. "You want me t'get you some?" he asked generously. "This is my second glass."

"Maybe later," Julie said. "Why don't you sit down here and we can get started."

Will grimaced. "Why do adults always use them re..."

"Rhetorical," Caleb supplied.

"Yeah, them. Ain't fair."

"As my grandmother used to say, God never promised that life would be fair, just that he would give you the strength to endure," Julie said.

To her surprise, Caleb burst into laughter.

"What's so funny about that?" she asked.

"It's not the sentiment. It's the relatives that the fates gifted us with. Your grandmother sounds like a female version of the judge. I wonder if such stoicism was the norm back then?"

"Don't care," Will muttered. "Don't even know what that word means."

"Stoicism means doing what needs to be done without a lot of complaining about doing it." She looked pointedly down at the math markers on the table.

"I didn't say I believed in it!" Will burst out.

"What is it you're teaching him?" Caleb asked.

"I'm *trying* to teach him set theory."

"Set theory! In first grade. He's too young."

"Ain't too young," Will grumbled. "Just ain't interested. And don't tell me bout them sto…thing."

"Maybe we ought to approach math from a different angle?" Caleb said slowly.

"Maybe we oughtn't to 'proach it a'tall." Will gave his opinion.

"What do you have in mind?" Julie asked Caleb. While Will needed to learn basic set theory, he did have all summer to do it, and, if Caleb had an idea that would incline the boy to view math as something less than torture, she was all for it.

"Maybe we ought to build a tree house," Caleb said.

"A tree house!" Will repeated. "You mean up in a tree? Off the ground?"

"Up a tree. Off the ground," Caleb clarified.

"Wow!" Will looked absolutely ecstatic.

"But Julie and I aren't going to do all the work," Caleb warned him. "I expect you to help with both the planning and the building."

"I will." The boy nodded his head vigorously in agreement.

"What do you think, Julie?" Caleb turned to her.

"I think it's a great idea," she said.

"Will, go out to the garage and get the large green tape measure that's hanging on the wall next to the hammers," Caleb told his son.

Will took off at a run, and Caleb turned to Julie.

"You really think it's a good idea?" he asked.

"I really do. On several fronts. All the measuring when you plan, and again when you build, is bound to help his math. Not only that, but it will give him some idea of what it is you do for a living."

And their working together would give Caleb and Will an opportunity to get to know each other better, she thought in satisfaction.

"Here it is!" Will came tearing back from the garage waving the tape measure in front of him. "What's we gonna do now?"

"Now we're going to figure out how big our tree house should be." Caleb took the tape from Will.

"Real big," Will suggested.

"How big we can make it depends on how much room we have to work with," Caleb told him. "The first step is to measure the length of those perpendicular limbs on the tree."

Julie studied the branches he was pointing to, mentally measured the distance from them to the ground, looked at Will who was dancing up and down with excitement and opted for safety.

"I think your father had better be the one to do the actual work in the tree. At least until he's been able to nail up some boards to provide a kind of safety net," she added at Will's disappointed look.

"Julie and I will take the preliminary measurements, son. Without something to hold on to, you really could fall and break something, and then you wouldn't be able to help me actually build the tree house."

Julie? Julie blinked. Since when had she volunteered to climb a tree?

"Someone has to hold the other end of the tape,"

Caleb said, having noticed her less than enthusiastic expression. "You aren't afraid of heights, are you?"

"No, only of falling off them."

"It's not her fault she's scared, Dad. She's a girl," Will whispered in an audible aside to Caleb.

Julie grimaced. "I swear that once they finally unravel all the DNA strands for men, they're going to find a gene for male chauvinism."

Will scowled. "Ain't nobody gonna unravel my parts."

Caleb laughed. "I wouldn't worry, son. From what I've seen, if there is any unraveling going on, you'll be the one doing it.

"Come on, Julie. Where's your sense of adventure?" Caleb teased.

"Cowering behind my common sense. Oh, all right," she capitulated beneath the twin pair of pleading eyes trained on her. "But I'm not climbing up that trunk. Actually—" she eyed the huge maple tree consideringly "—I don't think I could even if I wanted to."

"I'll get a ladder out of the garage," Caleb said.

"While your father is doing that, Will, let's get a diagram set up for you to record the measurements we call down to you," Julie said.

"Sure." Will rushed over to the table. He shoved the set-theory counters to one side and, grabbing a pencil, began to draw a credible replica of the tree.

"Very nice," Julie approved. "You seem to have inherited your father's talent for architecture."

"I wants to be like my great-grandfather," Will said. "The one who was a judge. Gonna make everyone do what they's supposed to."

For a moment, Will looked like a fragile lost child

and Julie's heart ached for him. His mother's casual desertion clearly bothered him more than he was willing to admit.

She leaned over and hugged his skinny little shoulders. ''You do that, Will. The world needs all the help it can get to behave right.''

To her surprise, Will fiercely returned her hug.

''I will. You wait and see.''

Julie looked down into his eyes, and for an eerie moment it was almost as if she was looking into Caleb's eyes. The grim determination mirrored there was identical.

Caleb's return with the ladder broke the poignant moment, and Julie turned to watch him position it securely against the tree.

He climbed up and down a couple of times and then announced, ''It's as safe as I can make it.''

''You're beginning to sound like a lawyer,'' Julie grumbled.

Caleb laughed. ''Sorry, it's in my genes.''

In his jeans? Julie's eyes instinctively dropped to his jeans. The softly worn fabric lovingly molded his body, and she swallowed uneasily as her imagination painted an erotic picture.

What was the matter with her? she wondered uneasily. She had never slipped into sensual fantasies about men before she'd met Caleb. She'd always acted like the levelheaded career woman she was. So why couldn't she seem to remember that when she was around Caleb?

She had no answer, and the fact worried her because if she didn't know why she was doing something, she couldn't change it. She had the oddest feeling that she'd ceded control of her emotions to a part of her mind that she hadn't even realized existed before.

"I'll go first so I can help you up," Caleb's deep voice broke into her muddled thoughts.

"Um, fine." Julie struggled to sound normal even though she was beginning to wonder what was normal for her anymore. Her whole personality seemed to be in a state of flux ever since she had met Caleb.

She watched admiringly as Caleb effortlessly sprinted up the ladder. He really was in good physical shape. He also seemed to be right at home scrambling around ladders.

A sudden shaft of fear pierced her at the thought of him climbing out onto the framework of a skyscraper to check on the construction process.

Caleb knows what he's doing, she tried to reason with her fear. Not only that, but he would hardly take any unnecessary risks. He took his responsibilities as a father far too seriously.

"Okay, come on up and watch your step," Caleb called down from above her.

"Here, Julie." Will handed her the tape measure.

Julie shoved it into her jeans pocket and, taking a deep steadying breath, cautiously climbed up the ladder.

"Take my hand to steady yourself," Caleb said, and Julie looked up to see his large hand in front of her. It looked strong. Capable of grabbing what it wanted and holding on to it.

Cautiously she let go of the ladder and reached up, feeling his fingers immediately close around her hand. A feeling of security slipped over her. She felt safe. As if nothing could harm her while he held her.

"There you go." Caleb pulled her the rest of the way up and then steadied her body against his.

Julie's eyes widened as she felt herself being pressed against the hard muscular length of him. She stared blindly at the creamy shirt button in the middle of his chest as she struggled to stamp out the sudden brushfire of desire that burned over her skin. It was impossible. Rational thought didn't stand a chance against the exquisite pleasure she could feel building in her.

She wanted to relax and let her much softer muscles mold themselves against his. She wanted to press her lips against the firm skin at the base of his neck. She wanted to touch that skin with the tip of her tongue.

She raised her head slightly and found her gaze locked onto his mouth. A wave of desire so strong she could almost taste it washed through her. Julie instinctively tensed, trying to control it.

"You okay, Julie?" Caleb demanded. "You really aren't afraid of heights, are you?"

"I'm fine." She put every ounce of firmness she could in her voice. "Just a little nervous at being off the ground," she offered, hoping he'd put down her abstracted manner to fear.

"There's nothing to worry about. I won't let anything happen to you," he said. "Just relax."

Caleb then made it impossible for her to relax when he put his arm around her waist to hold her anchored to the tree trunk and leaned around her to see where Will was.

"You ready to record the measurements, son?" Caleb called down, and his warm breath wafted across the back of her neck, sending goose bumps racing over her skin.

Julie stared blindly at the dark-brown bark of the tree and frantically concentrated on keeping her breathing even.

"Ready," Will called back.

Julie gulped as Caleb inched around her tense body and began to walk out along one of the tree's perpendicular limbs, using the branches above him to steady himself.

"Make sure the end of the measuring tape is flush with the trunk of the tree," Caleb told her, and Julie felt an irrational flash of anger at how normal he sounded. It didn't seem fair that she should be thrown so far off balance just by touching him, while he was totally unfazed.

"Fifty-six inches," Caleb called down.

"Fifty-six inches," Will repeated, and bent over his paper, laboriously copying the numbers.

Caleb then proceeded to work his way out on another limb, while Julie held her breath, praying he wouldn't slip and fall.

Ten minutes later, Caleb had finished measuring, and Julie scampered down the tree ahead of him. She didn't think she could contain her own emotions any longer if she had to stand still while he squeezed past her at the crotch of the tree one more time.

"I gots it all down!" Will waved the sheet of paper at Julie when she finally reached solid ground.

"Very good." She struggled to focus on his math. "Now, let's draw a diagram and label everything."

"I'll fix us a snack while you two do that," Caleb said. "All that tree climbing made me hungry."

"Fine," Julie said, glad of the chance to regain her emotional equilibrium.

An unexpected gust of anger shook Caleb at her calmness. How could she be unaffected by being pressed up against him, when he felt as if the imprint of her body had been seared into his flesh. Only the fact that Will had been standing below watching their every move had stopped him from doing something rash. Such as grabbing her and kissing her to relieve the unbearable tension that being close to her had generated.

Disgruntled, Caleb turned on his heel and headed to the kitchen. He had an appetite all right, but it sure wasn't for food.

Once in the kitchen, he dumped some of the chocolate chunk cookies they had made on a plate and opened the refrigerator to get the orange juice. His hand suddenly stilled as an idea hit him.

Tentatively he weighed it. It just might work, and at this point he was willing to try any long shot to gain a few minutes alone with her. Just a few seconds. That was all he needed. For now at least.

"Hey, Julie," he yelled out the back window to the patio. "Would you mind coming in here?"

"Just a second," she called back.

He watched in a rash of impatience as she pointed to something on the sheet in front of Will and said something that made the boy laugh.

Finally she got to her feet and headed into the house. To him.

"Finesse, Tarrington," he told himself, knowing even as he gave the order that he wouldn't be able to keep it. He wasn't a subtle man. And to further complicate matters, his need for Julie at this precise moment was so great it was clouding his normal good judgment. He grimaced. Just the fact that he was making up excuses to be alone with her for a few minutes was proof of that.

"Need help carrying things out?" Julie asked. "I'll get some glasses."

Glasses? He glanced down at his hand to find he was holding a carton of juice. He frowned. He didn't remember taking it out of the refrigerator.

He automatically gave her the carton when she held out her hand and then watched as she carefully filled the three glasses she'd gotten out of the cabinet.

"I'll take the plate of cookies and one glass, and you get the other two glasses, okay?" she said.

"Um, no," he stalled, frantically searching his mind for a sophisticated opening to broach what he really wanted. He didn't find anything even vaguely applicable.

"No?" Julie blinked. "Well, okay. Then you take the cookies and one glass, and I'll take the other two glasses."

"To hell with the damn cookies!" His frustration erupted.

Julie eyed Caleb uncertainly. His features seemed sharper somehow. As if he was in the grip of some strong emotion. A tiny spark of excitement began to burn under her breastbone. Was it possible he hadn't been unaffected by their closeness in the tree? Could he have felt even a fraction of the longing she had.

Unconsciously, she ran the tip of her tongue over her lower lip, and her excitement grew as his eyes followed the movement.

"What did you call me out here for if not to help carry the snack?" she asked.

"I...because...because I want to kiss you."

Julie swallowed on the sudden starburst of emotion that exploded in her. Caleb wanted to kiss her! Why he did she'd worry about later. For now, it was enough that he did.

When she didn't object, Caleb closed the short distance between them and, raising his hand, ran his fingertips over her cheek. The slightly roughened texture of his skin sent shivers of awareness skittering through her.

"Julie?" He paused as if waiting for her to say something, but at the moment she was incapable of a single word. Her whole being was focused on his mouth. On his firm lips. On her own longing to feel them.

Hoping that her silence meant assent, Caleb took her in his arms. He pulled her up against him, and a tremor started deep inside her, making her body feel pliable.

There was no reality for her beyond the fantastic sensations racing through her. Nothing in her life to date could even begin to compare with the excitement his lips caused.

Long before she had had a chance to fully savor the sensations filling her, Caleb dropped his arms and stepped back.

"Thanks, I needed that," he said, and then turned to pick up two of the glasses of orange juice.

But why had he needed that? Julie wanted to scream in frustration. Had he needed to kiss her because he needed to kiss *her,* Julie Raffet? Or had he needed it because he'd simply been aroused, and kissing any willing woman would have done? There was no possible way she could ask him without revealing just how deeply moving she had found his kiss. Which left her with yet one more unanswered question about Caleb.

With a sigh, she took the rest of their snack and followed Caleb out to the patio.

There were simply too many factors in their relationship that she couldn't get a handle on. Least of all, her own headlong response to Caleb Tarrington.

"Cookies! I's starved." Will's exuberant welcome to the food provided a welcome distraction.

Julie set the plate down on the table and reached for the paper Will had been copying his figures on.

"Once we've got the measurements, we can figure out how many boards we need to buy," Caleb said. "And what length..."

He paused as the phone rang inside the house.

"I'll get it," Will shouted, spraying cookie crumbs over the table. Without waiting for an answer, he raced into the house.

Julie had no more than dusted the crumbs off the table when he was back holding the cordless phone out in front of him.

"It's fer you." Will shoved the phone at Julie. "A man. He says his name's Joe, but he wouldn't tell me what he wants."

"One does not ask a caller why they want to speak to a guest," Caleb forced himself to correct Will's phone manners, when what he really wanted to do was to ask the boy if he'd found out anything else.

"Joe, what do you want?" Julie asked the question Caleb wanted to know. Unfortunately, he couldn't hear Joe's response, but it must have satisfied Julie because she simply murmured, "Sure, no problem."

Caleb felt his guts clench in rejection as she

laughed at something Joe said. He forced himself to ignore how he felt about the call in order to focus on what was being said. Or more important, how it was being said. Caleb suddenly realized something. Julie's tone of voice as she talked to Joe was the same one she used when she was explaining something to Will. There were none of the nuances that colored her voice when she was talking to him. But what did that all mean? he wondered. How could her relationship to Joe be on a par with her tutoring Will? Will was a kid, and Joe was a grown man.

Caleb didn't know. It was simply one more piece in the incredibly complex puzzle that was turning out to be Julie Raffet.

Chapter Eight

Caleb paused in the open doorway of his office, momentarily forgetting what he wanted to say as he caught sight of Julie.

She was seated at her desk, intently studying something on a sheet of paper. Her soft lips were slightly pursed as if she was concentrating, and Caleb felt a wave of desire unexpectedly slam through him. He wanted to kiss her delectable lips. To caress them until they were soft and pliable under his, and then he wanted...

His gaze slipped lower to linger on the slight swell of her breasts against the thin, white silk of her blouse. He took a deep breath, struggling to control his instinctive reaction.

"Did you want something?" The melodious sound of Julie's voice added a subtle thread to the texture of his thoughts.

Caleb swallowed as for one mad moment he considered answering her truthfully. Of telling her that, yes, he wanted something—her. He wanted to make love to her until her whole world comprised him and their lovemaking.

"Caleb?" A slight frown creased her forehead as he continued to simply stand there. "Are you okay?"

"Um, sorry. I was just thinking about something." He walked over to her desk. "Have you heard back from Maldon over at the site of the mall construction?"

"No. You want me to call him again?"

"Not yet. Give him until—" Caleb checked the wafer-thin gold watch on his wrist "—ten-thirty and then call. I need the figures he's supposed to get from the site foreman to take home with me, so I can work on them tonight."

"I can't call him at ten-thirty," Julie said.

Caleb sat down on the edge of her desk. "Why can't you call him at ten-thirty?"

Julie tried not to look at the way the taut material of his gray pants clearly outlined his muscular thigh.

"Because the chairman of the school hiring committee called a few minutes ago, and they want me to come by this morning for a few follow-up questions. If you don't mind, I'd like to leave here at ten-fifteen, and I probably won't be back until almost time to go to your house."

Caleb felt a flash of anger at the way the hiring committee kept jerking her around.

"You've already been interviewed and reinterviewed. Why don't you just write the committee off as an impossible bunch to please? It's not like you don't already have a job."

"I know, but this job is different." She leaned forward slightly in her anxiety to make him understand,

and it was all Caleb could do not to close the slight distance between them and kiss her.

Caleb stifled the urge and forced himself to maintain a politely attentive exterior while Julie listed in exhaustive detail all the reasons why the job at the charter school was so great.

Her eyes glowed and her soft cheeks were flushed with the strength of her enthusiasm. She...

Caleb's suddenly alert mind cut through his preoccupation with her physical appearance. That was it! From the very beginning, he'd sensed a difference between the way his ex-wife and Julie enthused about their careers. But he hadn't been able to figure out exactly what it was. Now he knew.

His ex-wife had always focused on how her career was going to advance her own personal goals. On what her career could do for her. Julie's total focus was on how she could use her career to make a difference in kids' lives. Julie saw her career as an opportunity to change the world around her. To make life better for kids.

Murna's focus was inward and Julie's was outward, probably because Julie was a very giving person, while his ex-wife had been a taker.

Not only that, Caleb realized, but Julie looked at her career very much the way he viewed his own. He didn't feel he was just throwing up buildings. He felt he was creating structures that were both aesthetically pleasing and necessary to the smooth functioning of society. He felt the same sense of accomplishment at designing a well-built, much-used shopping mall as Julie did when she was able to teach a student to read.

"Sorry," Julie muttered at his abstracted expression. "I tend to get carried away with my enthusiasm."

"No more than I do about my designs. I..." He paused when he noticed what was written on the sheet of paper she had been studying. It was filled with numbers. Small numbers. Certainly nothing to do with work.

"What is this?" he asked curiously.

"Just something personal." She hastily stuffed the paper into her desk drawer.

Caleb thoughtfully studied her embarrassed expression.

"Your car?" He guessed.

"I was just seeing if I could juggle things to find a way to make payments on one," she admitted.

"And?" he asked.

Julie sighed. "The only way it can be done is if I were to withdraw from the two graduate classes I'm registered for this summer, and I need those classes. Besides, even if I did that, I'd have to wait till the university got around to processing a refund check and that could take months. Literally."

Caleb felt a deep sense of frustration. She needed a car, and he could buy one for her out of petty cash and never even notice it. And yet he couldn't. She would never take it from him. But maybe... A glimmer of an idea occurred to him.

"You said November was when you would be able to afford payments?"

"Yes."

"Suppose I were to make the payments on a car for you until November and then you can take them over?"

"No." Julie instinctively rejected the idea of taking money from him.

"Listen to me a minute before you refuse," he said. "You are spending the summer tutoring Will, to say nothing of helping me here until Miss Andrews can get back. My making your car payments for a few months doesn't begin to cover what you've done for me."

"But I didn't ask you for any money," Julie insisted.

"How do you make your living?" Caleb demanded.

She frowned, not seeing the connection.

"I teach."

"And how do I make my living?" he rushed on before she could say anything else.

"You design things."

"True. And if someone came into my office and asked me to design a house for them, and they were well able to afford to pay for it, would you expect me to do the work for nothing?"

"Of course not, but you are going to design the playground."

"No, a member of my staff will, and the firm will take a tax write-off. I asked you to teach my son. I am perfectly capable of paying for it. Actually, I would prefer to pay for it because then we're equals."

Julie blinked, caught off guard by his logic. She'd been so determined not to take anything from him that it had never occurred to her to consider the situation from his point of view.

"Exactly what are you offering?" she asked slowly.

"To make your car payments through October as

repayment for your tutoring Will,'' Caleb said, holding his breath as she considered his idea.

''I have the feeling there's a fallacy in your argument, but I can't figure out what it is. So I accept your offer,'' she said, hoping she was doing the right thing, and not just the easy thing.

''Good.'' Caleb hurriedly changed the subject before she changed her mind.

''How are you planning on getting to your interview this morning?'' Caleb asked.

''I'll call a taxi.''

''Don't bother.'' Caleb stood up and pulled his key ring out of his pocket. ''Take my car. You know where it's parked.''

He dropped the keys on her desk, and Julie stared at the tangle of metal. It looked like an abstract sculpture, but what it really was was a puzzle. Why was he letting her drive his car? It probably cost more than her house had. Not only that, but every man she'd ever met had been very possessive of his car, and yet here was Caleb casually handing her the keys to his as if...

As if what? As if he cared about her comfort? Or as if he wanted her back at the office as quickly as possible? She had no idea.

''There's a problem?'' Caleb asked.

''Not exactly.'' She tentatively poked the silver keys with her finger. ''It's just that your car is very expensive. What happens if I dent a fender?''

''I get it fixed. You may name your car and give it a personality, Julie, but as far as I'm concerned, a car is just a mechanical device. Like that computer you're using.''

"Then thank you. I appreciate it." Julie accepted his offer in the same casual manner he'd extended it.

"As for Maldon, you'd better call him now and tell him to drop the figures I need by my house on his way home this evening."

He headed back to his office. Pausing in the doorway, he turned and added, "And let me know before you leave."

"Of course."

A little over an hour later, Julie finished the last letter she had to do, covered the computer and got to her feet. She hurried into the washroom off her office and quickly washed the ink from the printer from her fingers.

She ran a quick comb through her gleaming hair, put on fresh lipstick and then brushed any stray hairs off the jacket of her kelly-green linen blazer. She nodded her head with satisfaction. She looked both professional and cheerful. An image that any elementary teacher wanted to project.

Hurrying back into her office, she grabbed her purse and Caleb's car keys.

"All set to go?" Caleb asked when she entered his office.

"Yes. I'm off to beard the lion in his den, as it were."

Caleb chuckled, and Julie's stomach twisted at the engaging sound.

She watched as he approached, her heart rate accelerating the closer he got.

It became a drumbeat in her ears when he finally came to a halt scant inches from her.

Mesmerized, she watched as he raised his hand, and gently caressed her cheek.

"Wh—" To her dismay her voice broke. Quickly firming it, she went on. "What are you doing?"

"I'm going to kiss you for luck," Caleb said.

"Luck?" The word came out in a squeak.

"Don't knock it."

Julie's breath caught in her throat as she felt his arms close around her.

"A body needs all the luck in this world it can get." His arms tightened slightly, pulling her closer and sending her heart into her throat.

To heck with what a body needed, Julie thought distractedly. What her body wanted was to be closer to Caleb. To be able to feel the imprint of his each individual muscle.

Her eyelids felt weighed by the force of her desire. When his mouth finally covered hers, Julie felt as if a dozen sparklers had gone off behind her eyelids. As if the tiny sparks were burning away her inhibitions. She swayed forward slightly, unable to stand beneath the onslaught of feeling that tore through her, and his arms tightened as he deepened the kiss.

Long moments later, Caleb lifted his head and stared down at her. His eyes seemed to glow as if lit from within and the muscles in his face were sharply etched as if he shared some of the tension twisting through her.

Dropping one last kiss on her soft lips, he said, "You go, girl."

"Why?" she muttered.

"Because you want the job."

"No, why do you keep kissing me?" Julie blurted out, frustrated at her inability to figure out why a sophisticated man like Caleb Tarrington kept kissing an ordinary school teacher like her.

"Because you have soft, delectable lips that are eminently kissable. Because you are an incredibly sensual bundle of femininity that fits perfectly into my arms, and because kissing you is a fantastic mood elevator," he said.

And because if I did what I really wanted to, which would be to snatch you up in my arms, carry you off somewhere and make mad, passionate love to you, you'd run like crazy and never speak to me again, he thought ruefully.

"Oh," Julie murmured as his enchanting words floated through her mind. It wasn't just a case of Caleb kissing an available woman. Caleb wanted to kiss her. Julie Raffet. Personally.

Picking up her purse, she left the office feeling as if she were floating. Everything in her whole world was perfect at that moment.

She smiled at a strange man getting off the elevator as she got on, not even noticing when he turned to take a second look at her through the closing elevator doors. As far as she was concerned, there was no other man of interest in the whole world except Caleb Tarrington. He was absolutely perfect. Not only was he perfect, but his kisses were the embodiment of her every fantasy. He...

Her euphoric mood came to a crashing end as she suddenly realized why she felt that way. She was in love with Caleb Tarrington!

The appalling revelation slammed through her with the force of a blow, and Julie instinctively put out her hand to steady herself on the brass rail that encircled the elevator.

No, she tried to argue with her unwanted flash of insight. She wasn't in love with him. She was…she desperately scrambled to find a non-threatening explanation. She was…in like. That was it. She liked Caleb Tarrington. Just liked him.

Julie sighed in defeat as the words echoed mockingly through her mind. Lying to herself wasn't going to help the situation.

"I am in love with Caleb Tarrington," she informed the control panel of the empty elevator. "I am head over heels in love with Caleb Tarrington. I am an absolute fool," she added, but even the sure knowledge that she was right made no difference to how she felt.

Her mind might know that there was no future in loving Caleb, but her heart wasn't so sure. After all, Prince Charming had married Cinderella. It was possible.

The elevator doors opened with a quiet whir, and Julie got out. This definitely wasn't the time to worry about her feelings for Caleb. Right now she had to drive a strange car across town, and once she got there, she was going to have to try to sell both herself and her ideas on education to the hiring committee. That had to be her primary focus, she told herself. Afterward she would consider what she should do about her love for Caleb.

Unfortunately, Julie's interview did nothing to restore her peace of mind, and by the time she got back to Caleb's office she was a bundle of frustrated nerves.

Caleb took one look at her rigid features and took the keys out of her fingers and her purse out of her hand. He dropped the keys in his pocket and tossed her purse on her desk.

Placing his hands on her slender shoulders, he turned her around and began to gently massage her tense muscles.

"It isn't the car that's upset you, so what did?"

"How do you know it isn't the car?" She sighed as his strong fingers began to loosen her stiff muscles.

"Because I know you. If you'd put a dent in the car, you'd look guilty. You don't look guilty, you look mad as hell. So I assume it had something to do with the interview."

Julie grimaced.

"Dead on. I all but told one of the members of the committee that not only was she an idiot, but a bigoted one in the bargain!"

Caleb chuckled. "Then I assume she was. Which undoubtedly means you were better off coming out with the truth rather than implying it, because idiots never pick up on hints. Tell me, what did this particular idiot do?"

"This particular idiot is of the opinion that simply because a kid comes from an economically deprived background, they are also intellectually incapable of learning! Can you imagine?" Julie's voice rose with the strength of her anger.

"Kids from poor backgrounds are every bit as capable of learning as those who come from wealthy backgrounds. They may be lacking in some of the background stuff that most kids today pick up in preschool, but that doesn't mean that they can't learn and learn every bit as well as their peers from the suburbs!"

"Relax..." Caleb's soothing voice flowed over her

retightening muscles. "You don't have to convince me. Remember, I have one of the kids who didn't learn all the stuff suburban moms seem to feel it's their duty to pass on to their offspring."

Julie was too angry to respond. She felt as if she was about to explode from the force of her indignation.

"I couldn't believe it! That numskull woman, who has the audacity to call herself a teacher, is the reason why the committee keeps calling and asking me more questions. She feels that I would be too demanding on children from underprivileged backgrounds!"

"What are you going to do?" Caleb asked, and the question caught her off guard.

Her righteous anger began to dissipate somewhat as she considered his question. Caleb wasn't trying to tell her what she should do. Instead, he was paying her the compliment of treating her like a rational adult who could make her own decisions.

She was momentarily distracted when Caleb dropped his hands and stepped back.

"I don't know," she said. "But I'm open to suggestions."

Caleb felt a sense of satisfaction at her willingness to listen to him.

"Does this hiring committee have the final word?" he asked.

"On paper, no. The actual hiring is done by the school board, but in reality all the board will do is rubber-stamp the committee's recommendations."

"Have you tried talking to this woman one-on-one?"

Julie snorted. "One doesn't talk to her, one talks *at* her. From what I've seen, she has some kind of mental filter that screens out anything she doesn't want to hear. What she needs is a good swift smack upside the head!''

Caleb chuckled. ''Bloodthirsty wench. If you decide to do it, let me know in advance so I can have your bail money ready.''

Julie grimaced. ''It would almost be worth it. I can't think of a single thing to do about her. I've already tried confronting her, but she won't argue facts and studies, she argues compassion. As if it were compassionate to treat poor kids as second-class learners. And contacting the other members of the committee privately would be seen as going behind her back, and that would brand me as not a team player.''

''I think this is the time for one of the judge's sayings,'' Caleb said.

''All right, I'll bite. What did the judge say about this situation?''

''When you have done everything you can do to solve a problem, walk away from it. Either your efforts will resolve it or they won't, but continuing to dwell on it is a waste of both your time and mental energy.''

Julie grimaced. ''Physically, I already have walked away. It's the mental distancing that I am having trouble with. Did he have any advice on how to do that?''

''Focus on something else,'' Caleb said.

Julie squinted slightly as she considered the idea. ''It's not working. I keep thinking about what I'd like to do with the woman, and none of it is legal, let alone moral.''

Caleb saw the shadow that darkened her eyes and wanted to banish it. ''It's too bad this isn't one of your fairy tales," he said. "You could sure use a knight on a white charger riding to the rescue."

A soft smile unconsciously curved her lips. Caleb would make a perfect knight.

"Actually, what I really need is a villain to spirit that blasted woman away somewhere until after the hiring is done," she said. "And villains are a lot harder to control."

"The judge didn't think so," Caleb said.

"Yeah, but he had help. There's never a court bailiff around when you need one. I guess I'll just have to do my best to put it out of my mind for the time being."

"You really want that job, don't you?" Caleb felt an intense sense of her frustration. He wanted to do something to help her. To make her world right, and yet he couldn't. Even if he had the contacts, which he didn't, Julie would resent him using them on her behalf.

Julie nodded. "I really want that job, but I'm going to try to take the judge's advice and put it out of my mind."

"Then, let's get out of here," Caleb said. "It'll be easier to forget them at home."

"True." Julie got her gym bag out of the closet, while Caleb retrieved his briefcase from his office.

"By the way, Miss Andrews called while you were gone. Her mother is doing much better and is coming home from the hospital tomorrow. After that, it's simply a matter of making sure that the nurse Miss Andrews hired to live with her mother works out. With any luck, she should be back here by the middle of next week."

Julie ignored the sense of loss she felt at the realization that her mornings of working with Caleb were numbered in favor of trying to find out more about the perfect Miss Andrews while she had the chance.

"Is her mother expected to make a full recovery?" Julie asked.

Caleb pushed the elevator button for the ground floor and then said, "I'm not sure, but she seems to be doing pretty well for a woman of almost ninety."

"Ninety!" Julie repeated in surprise. If her mother was ninety, then Miss Andrews must be...

"Uh-huh. She celebrated her eighty-third birthday shortly after Miss Andrews came to work for me, and that was more than six years ago."

"How old is Miss Andrews?" Julie asked.

Caleb grinned. "My guess would be somewhere in her mid-fifties, but I have better sense than to ask. You'll see what I mean when you meet her. Miss Andrews is not the kind of woman one takes liberties with."

"I'm looking forward to it," Julie said sincerely. Now that she knew Miss Andrews was old enough to be Caleb's mother, she was prepared to like her every bit as much as he did.

"I called down to the office while you were gone and asked if anyone knew of a good used-car lot," Caleb said once they were in his Mercedes. "You'll get better value for your money with a used car."

"Any luck?" Julie asked.

"Yes, Dave said that his brother-in-law has a used-car lot and is very careful to only sell reliable cars."

"Which would help," Julie said. "I wouldn't know a lemon unless it wore a sign."

"I'll look it over for you," Caleb said. "We can

stop on our way home and see what he's got on his lot."

"Sounds good," Julie agreed.

Ten minutes later, Caleb pulled into the used-car lot and parked in front of the showroom. Julie climbed out of the car and looked around with interest. There were several dozen vehicles neatly parked in the lot.

"May I help you?" A short, slightly overweight man eyed Caleb's Mercedes as if wondering what a man who could afford to drive a car like that was doing in a used-car lot.

Caleb didn't say anything, allowing Julie to respond, a fact that pleased her enormously.

"Yes, sir, I'm looking for a used car that's in good shape, and that I can afford," Julie succinctly stated her needs.

"I only sell reliable cars," the man said. "In this business I have to depend on repeat customers, and if I sell them a lemon, they sure aren't going to come back. As to cost, I'm sure we can come up with a finance plan that you can afford." He shot another curious glance at Caleb's S-class Mercedes.

Julie ignored his curiosity. She had no intention of explaining her relationship with Caleb to a stranger. Besides, she wasn't sure exactly what it was herself.

"I'm Bart Machineski, and you are…"

"Raffet, Julie Raffet, and this is Caleb Tarrington." She gestured toward Caleb.

"Mr. Tarrington." The man shook Caleb's hand with enthusiasm. "Dave called me not thirty minutes ago to say you might be bringing a friend by to look over our cars. Don't you worry about a thing. I promised Dave I'd take good care of the little lady."

Julie bit back an instinctive protest at being labeled a "little lady." A frustrating experience had long ago convinced her that trying to reform chauvinistic strangers was a total waste of time. And Caleb... Julie shot a quick glance at his face as he listened to something the salesman was saying about their mutual acquaintance, Dave. Caleb didn't need reforming. He had shown himself perfectly willing to treat her as an intelligent human being capable of handling her own affairs.

"Now then, Miss Raffet—" the salesman turned to Julie "—I have several cars, including a really nice station wagon I just got in that might interest you. All are rust free, under twenty thousand miles and have been well maintained by their owners. All still have part of the factory warranty on them."

"A station wagon? Could I see it?" she asked.

"Sure, it's right over here," Bart said.

Julie fell into step behind the salesman with Caleb bringing up the rear.

"What do you think?" Bart asked once she'd looked the car over.

"It certainly seems nice," she said slowly.

"Why don't you take it for a test drive to see if you like the way it handles," Caleb suggested.

Julie checked her watch. "I don't have time right now," she said. "I want to get back to Will. If we stay any later, he'll be wondering where we are."

"Tell you what, Miss Raffet," Bart said. "I'll knock five hundred off the asking price if you have a car to trade in."

"I have a car, but it isn't running," Julie said.

"Doesn't matter, we can use it for parts," Bart said.

"Then I just need to call the credit union and find out what the payments would be," Julie said.

"Tell you what. I'll hold the car for you for forty-eight hours with no strings attached. Just give me a call, and let me know if you'll be coming in to test-drive it, okay?"

"Very okay." Julie smiled happily at the man.

"Good. Here's my business card with my phone number on it. Someone will be here until eight this evening. Just leave a message if I'm not here."

"Thank you for your help." Julie shook his hand and then stepped back so that Caleb could do the same.

"Glad to be of service," Bart said seriously. "I've found that if you treat people fairly, they not only come back for other cars, but they tell their friends about you. A satisfied customer is the best advertising in the world."

"I don't doubt it," Julie said as they walked back to Caleb's car.

"If you get a favorable answer from your credit union, I can pick you up tomorrow morning so you can test-drive the station wagon. Unless you have something planned for Saturday?" Caleb said.

"Nothing," Julie said, ignoring the thousand and one things around the house she should be doing. Not a one of them began to compare with the pleasure of spending time with Caleb. "I appreciate your help."

"Like Bart, I'm glad to be of service."

No, Julie thought, Caleb wasn't like Bart at all. Caleb was in a class all by himself. As far as she was concerned, Caleb represented the pinnacle of masculine perfection. He was Prince Charming, Sir Lancelot and a whole host of other heroes all rolled up into one delectable man. She stifled a sigh. She just wished he thought of her as being someone special. But he did like to kiss her. And she drew what comfort she could from the indisputable fact, even if she didn't understand it.

"What's the matter?" Caleb asked as he pulled into his driveway.

"Nothing." Julie hastily banished the thought. There was a lot to enjoy about what she did have with Caleb. Better to savor that and not worry because she didn't have everything she wanted, she told herself. Very few people got their every wish fulfilled. Or even most of them for that matter.

"I wonder where Will is." Caleb looked around at the deserted backyard as they entered the house.

They found him almost immediately. Will was sprawled on the floor in the recreation room watching television.

"Uh-oh," Caleb muttered. "I should have told Miss Vincent to keep the television off."

"A highly impractical approach," Julie said. "Better to just monitor what he watches."

Caleb grimaced. "I wouldn't know one television show from another. I only have that thing because Miss Vincent is a big fan of the soaps, and she only agreed to work for me if I bought one for her."

"No problem. I'm pretty up on the subject. I'll see what he's watching."

"Okay, you do that and I'll tell Miss Vincent we're here," Caleb said, relieved to leave the problem in Julie's capable hands.

"Hello, son," Caleb told the absorbed Will as he passed the boy.

Will gave a grunt, but whether it was in greeting

or in annoyance that his television watching had been interrupted, Julie didn't know.

Julie sat down in the chair behind Will and looked at the screen, relaxing slightly when she recognized the show. Will wasn't going to pick up any antisocial ideas from *Leave It To Beaver*.

"Any good?" she asked once a commercial had come on.

Will rolled over and studied her for a long moment and then announced. "You know, you's just like the Beaver's mom."

Julie blinked in surprise. As far as she was concerned, the only resemblance she bore to June Cleaver was their gender.

"How so?" Julie asked cautiously.

"You listen," Will said seriously. "Just like she does. You really listen to what I say."

"That's true." Julie felt a flash of tenderness at Will's earnest expression.

"My mom, she's not like Beaver's mom. My mom, she don't never listen. Not even when she's looking straight at me. But you do."

Leave it to a child to cut through all the supercilious stuff and realize what was so special about June Cleaver. What made her a good mom. Not because she spent her days cleaning the house in high heels, a dress and pearls, or because she always seemed to have homemade cookies on hand. No, what made June Cleaver special was that she listened to her kids.

"I wish you was my mom." Will's muttered comment shook Julie to her core. Mainly because it so closely paralleled the direction of her thoughts recently. She wanted to tell him that she wished she was his mother too, but she couldn't. He didn't need to build a future on empty dreams.

Fortunately, Will didn't seem to expect an answer. He turned back to his show.

"Don't start to watch anything else," Julie said as she got to her feet. "I'm going to change clothes, and as soon as this is over, we'll start work."

"I won't," Will promised. "Some guy delivered a whole pile of boards and stuff this morning. It's out back. So's we can build the tree house. That's more fun than television."

Julie shivered as she remembered the last time she'd been up a tree with Caleb. Fun didn't begin to describe the experience.

Chapter Nine

Caleb felt his spirits soar as he pulled into Julie's driveway Saturday afternoon. Just being around Julie was the best mood elevator he'd ever found. Although he had the unsettling feeling that as a mood elevator Julie's presence could be addictive. Too long without seeing her made him feel faintly uneasy. As if something vital was missing from his life.

Caleb pushed the implications of the disquieting thought to the back of his mind as he crossed the small patch of lawn to her front porch. The inside door was standing wide open, and he peered through the screen door into the living room. She wasn't to be seen.

"Julie," he called. "It's me. Caleb."

Julie's head jerked around at the sound of Caleb's voice. He certainly didn't need to identify himself, she thought ruefully. The dark velvety texture of his voice was unique. She'd recognize his voice if she never heard it again until her dying day. It was indelibly imprinted on her heart.

She tossed her pen on top of her bank statement, which she'd been attempting to balance, and jumped to her feet, eager not to waste a moment now that Caleb was here.

She hurried out of her small study into the living room.

"Come in," she called through the open door.

He stepped inside and then demanded, "Have you no common sense, woman!"

"And a good morning to you, too," Julie said.

"That screen door wasn't locked."

Julie chuckled. "What was your first clue, Sherlock? The fact that I told you to come in, or the fact that there was no resistance when you pulled on the door?"

Caleb fought not to allow the enticing sound of her laughter to distract him.

"It isn't funny!" he insisted.

"You couldn't tell by me. I don't understand enough of what's going on to make a valid judgment."

"Leaving your door open is an invitation to every thief and murderer in town."

Julie blinked. "We haven't had a murder in this town for well over a hundred years."

"That's not to say that we won't have one. You need to keep your doors locked."

"In broad daylight?" Julie objected. "Next you'll be telling me I should get myself a gun."

Caleb felt a trickle of icy fear slither through him at the very thought of Julie with a gun. She'd never be able to shoot someone, even if that someone was trying to hurt her. An intruder would just take the gun away and use it against her.

"No, I'm not suggesting that you get a gun. Guns are damn dangerous in the hands of amateurs."

"From what I've seen, they aren't any too safe in the hands of experts either," Julie muttered.

Caleb refused to be sidetracked. "In this day and age, a person has to take reasonable precautions. This screen door wouldn't keep out a prepubescent mugger."

"Hmm. Step outside a minute," Julie said.

"Okay," Caleb said, hoping that she was beginning to understand the danger she was inadvertently courting.

Once he was back on the porch, Julie closed the screen door behind him and then the outside door.

Caleb listened to the sound of the dead-bolt lock clicking into place. He waited a long moment and, when nothing happened, yelled through the door, "What are you doing?"

"You told me to keep people out, and once I start suspecting every passing stranger of having designs on my person or my property, I could get so paranoid I think everyone is suspect."

"Julie, open this damn door!"

"But, Caleb, how can I trust you? For all I know, you might have suddenly turned into a monster overnight. Or maybe you've been possessed by aliens."

"Maybe you've lost your mind!"

"Me? I wasn't the one who was seeing murderers behind every tree." The laughter threaded through her voice made him want to grab her and shake some sense into her head, and then he wanted to kiss her senseless. Once he got his hands on her...

But how? was the question. He studied the solid oak outer door. Not through there. Sears hadn't stinted on the strength of their front doors, but maybe…

Pretending to have given up, he casually walked off the porch and started around the house as if he was going to his car. Once he reached the driveway, he sprinted toward the back door. If he knew Julie, her back door would be as wide open as her front one had been.

Julie heard the sound of his pounding feet and, realizing what he was up to, raced through the house, trying to reach the back door first. She got to it at the same time he did. Grabbing the handle on the screen door, she tried to keep him from pulling it open.

It didn't work. Caleb was stronger. Much stronger. She felt herself inexorably being pulled forward.

"Yes?" Caleb said when he had the door entirely open. "Now what do you plan on doing?"

"Julie?" an elderly voice called from over the fence on the side lot. "Is that man bothering you? You want me to call the cops?"

Julie looked up into Caleb's surprised face. He certainly did bother her on just about every level of her existence. But if her own common sense couldn't talk her out of loving him, then the police certainly couldn't do anything about it.

"It's okay, Gus. This is Caleb Tarrington, a friend of mine who was trying to convince me to barricade myself behind locked doors because of all the nuts running loose in the world."

"This ain't the world, young man!" Gus fixed Caleb with a baleful glare. "This here's our neighborhood, and we look out for one another. Ain't no shenanigans going to get by us. And don't you forget it, neither!''

"No, sir," Caleb said. "It's a comfort to know that Julie's neighbors look after her."

"No more'n she'd do for me." Gus nodded, and slowly made his way back to his house.

"Admit you're wrong," Julie said.

"I am not wrong, but I am impressed that your neighbor was willing to interfere on your behalf. Especially one that old. In my neighborhood, people rely on security systems instead of each other."

"Our way is better." Julie let go of the screen door and stepped aside so Caleb could come back.

"We'll argue it out another time," Caleb said, not willing to give up. Julie's safety was far too important. He'd just have to think of a more convincing argument.

"At the moment, getting you some transportation is more important," Caleb continued. "You ready to go test-drive that wagon you saw yesterday?"

"Yes," Julie said.

"Have you got the title to your car in case you do decide to buy a new one and want to trade it in?"

"The title?" she repeated.

"You'll need it to transfer your old car to the dealer."

Julie frowned slightly.

"What's the problem?" Caleb asked when she continued to simply stand there. "Don't you know where it is?"

"Of course I know where it is. It's in a safe place. I'm just not too clear on which safe place I put it in."

She glanced vaguely around the room as if seeking inspiration.

"How many safe places do you have?" Caleb asked curiously.

"Lots," she admitted. "And some of them are so safe no one has ever found them again, including me."

"You don't have a file box filled with warranties and the like?"

"No," she murmured absently. "I keep meaning to sort through things and organize everything, but somehow I always seem to get sidetracked."

When Caleb didn't say anything, Julie looked at him. "What, no comment?"

"Not hardly. After all, Will and I are two of the things that sidetracked you. I'd much rather have you the way you are than organized and not having the time to help us."

"Thank you," she said, warmed by his words.

"So where do we start looking?" he asked.

"My desk drawer, I guess."

She went into her small office and, yanking out the middle drawer, carried it back into the living room where she emptied it onto the floor.

Caleb looked from the thin drawer to the huge pile of papers on the floor and said, "Impressive. You've defied the laws of physics."

She grinned at him. "It's a talent schoolteachers develop early."

Dropping to the floor beside the pile, she began to sift through it.

"We could organize this stuff into piles, and you could file the piles when you get time," he suggested. "It wouldn't take any longer than sorting through it."

"Okay," Julie accepted. "Let's sort by bills, warranties, personal letters and other."

"Can do." Caleb picked up a stack and began to sift through it. They were halfway through the pile when the front door suddenly burst open to reveal a large man holding a huge bouquet of flowers.

"Julie, I will love you to my dying day!" the man announced.

Caleb took one look at the man's idiotic grin and wanted to shove it down his throat. If this didn't prove his point about the dangers of leaving the door unlocked, he didn't know what did. How dare this guy just barge into Julie's house and...

And what? Caleb suddenly wondered. What did the guy want? He shot a quick glance at Julie to see how she was taking this.

With a total lack of reaction, he realized in surprise. She didn't seem overjoyed at either the man's announcement or his presence. She seemed to be...

Caleb studied her mobile features. Amused, he finally decided. Julie appeared to be amused by her visitor. Surely if this guy were a romantic interest of hers, she wouldn't find him amusing. Caleb started to relax slightly and then stiffened again when he remembered how she'd laughed at his attempt to get her to lock her door.

Getting to her feet, Julie said, "Hi, Joe. I take it you met with success?"

Joe gave her a hearty kiss that made Caleb furious. He'd always thought that the expression *seeing red* was simply poetic license on the part of writers. Now he knew better. He was viewing Joe through a pinkish haze that seemed to shimmer. It took every ounce of willpower Caleb had to keep from physically yanking Julie out of Joe's arms. How dare he touch her. Julie was his. She was an essential part of him. Because he loved her. The unexpected revelation was a body blow that sent him reeling mentally. Grimly he fought to stay focused in the present. Later he could worry about the implications of his self-discovery.

"Caleb, my impetuous visitor is Joe Valuchi. Joe, this is Caleb Tarrington."

"Hey there, Caleb." Joe nodded pleasantly at him before turning back to Julie.

"The answer is yes!" he announced.

"What was the question?" Caleb said tightly.

Julie shot a quick glance at Caleb, wondering why he sounded so short. Joe's enthusiasm was sometimes hard to take, but he was essentially harmless. And she should know. She'd been his friend since kindergarten.

"The question was, 'Margie, will you marry me?'" Joe's features took on a besotted look.

Caleb fought his way to the surface of the relief that flooded him and asked, "Who's Margie?"

"The woman of his dreams," Julie enlightened him. "I've been giving Joe advice on how to court her."

"Margie is the most wonderful woman the good Lord ever created," Joe elaborated. "And she's all mine."

"Congratulations," Caleb said sincerely. He didn't know who Margie was, and he didn't care. As long as Julie didn't figure into any of Joe's future plans, he wished the guy every happiness.

"I can't stay," Joe told Julie. "I'm meeting Margie this morning, and we're going to pick out a ring. I just wanted to bring you some flowers and give you the good news. You're a real sport, Julie."

A real sport? Caleb blinked in disbelief at Joe's

description. Was the man blind? Julie was the most seductive, most alluring woman he'd ever seen, and Joe called her a sport?

"Bye, Julie." Joe suddenly remembered he was still holding the flowers and shoved them at her. "And it was nice to meet you…"

"Caleb Tarrington," Caleb reminded him.

"Yeah." Joe nodded, and with one more grin at Julie, left.

"I'd better put these in water," Julie said.

Caleb followed Julie out into the kitchen, intensely curious about her reaction to Joe's news. On the surface, it didn't seem as if she cared, but then looks could be deceiving. A fact he knew only too well.

"I wonder if he'll be happy with Margie?" Caleb probed.

Julie carefully put the extravagant bouquet into a vase of water to keep it fresh until she could find the time to arrange it properly.

"I haven't the foggiest," she said. "I've never met his Margie."

"Aren't you worried that he might be making a mistake by marrying her?"

"Nope," Julie said. "Joe's a grown man. He said she was the one for him and, if she isn't, then he's the one who is going to have to deal with it. I don't screen my friends' romantic interests."

"Very wise." Caleb felt himself relaxing. Julie couldn't be nursing a hidden love for Joe. She'd never be able to talk about him so casually if she were. That was one less thing he had to worry about.

"There." Julie set the vase of flowers on the counter. "Where were we?"

"Looking for the title to your car," Caleb told her.

"And not having any success." She went back into the living room. "Do you know what a title looks like?"

Caleb tried to remember what the title to his car looked like.

"Official," he finally said.

"Official?" Julie stared off into the middle distance. "Maybe I put it with my teaching certificates."

She hurried back into her office and went into the closet. Taking a brown cardboard folder down from the shelf, she opened it and pulled out a handful of documents.

"They certainly look official," Caleb agreed, staring at the large state seal on the top one.

"I think..." She ruffled through the papers, pausing as she got about halfway through.

"Eureka!" she announced. "One car title."

Caleb took the sheet she held out and read it.

"One car title," he agreed. "Let's go."

"Sure." She grabbed her purse and stuffed the title in it. "You go out through the kitchen and pull the door closed behind you. That'll lock it, and I'll get the front door. It takes a key."

"So you do lock doors occasionally?" He couldn't resist the comment.

"Of course I do. Simply because I refuse to allow the nuts in this world to force me to live in a state of siege doesn't mean I don't take precautions when I'm not here."

Caleb headed toward the kitchen to lock the back door, feeling slightly better. She might be a little too trusting for today's world, but, at least, she wasn't stupidly trusting.

* * *

The used-car salesman came out to meet them when Caleb parked in front of the showroom.

"Good morning, Mr. Tarrington, Ms. Raffet. Ready to give that wagon a test drive, Ms. Raffet?"

"Yes." Julie noticed that the car was now parked in front of the office. "Is someone else interested in it?"

"No, I simply brought it around front to save time. It's a great car though. I won't have any trouble selling it. Here's the keys, take all the time you need to make up your mind."

It didn't take Julie much time at all. Once around the block and she was sold.

"You like it?" Caleb asked from the passenger's side.

"What's not to like? Not only does it handle well, but it's got lots of storage in the back. I'll be able to lug all kinds of things back and forth to school."

And it was solidly built, Caleb thought with satisfaction. It would provide her with some measure of protection in case of an accident.

Once back on the lot, the car salesman was able to complete the paperwork very quickly, and forty minutes later, Julie was happily following Caleb to his home in her new used car.

She turned into Caleb's driveway to find Will dancing up and down on the grass in an agony of impatience.

"Hey, Julie," he yelled as he raced over to her once she'd turned off the car. "Where ya been? I's been waitin' and waitin.'"

"Hey, Will!" She gave him a quick hug. "I've been to market to buy a—"

"Fat pig!" Will finished the nursery rhyme for her and then burst into laughter.

Caleb looked from his son to Julie and then said, "What are you two talking about?"

"It's a literary allusion," Julie said.

"Yeah." Will chortled, inordinately pleased to have understood something his father hadn't. "It's a lit...what she said."

"From a nursery rhyme," she elaborated at Caleb's blank expression.

"Can I drive your car, Julie?" Will asked.

"No!" Julie and Caleb spoke in unison.

"Why not?"

"Because you can't see over the dashboard for one thing and, for another, it's illegal." Caleb made the fatal mistake of trying to reason with a six-year-old.

"But the judge, he's dead. You said so. I remember."

"The law isn't dead, even if it does occasionally seem that it's on life support," Caleb said.

"But—" Will began.

"You may not drive, steer or in any way operate any car until you are sixteen," Julie said flatly.

"But—"

"Period. This subject is not open for negotiation," Julie said.

"Aw sh..." Will hastily backtracked when he saw his father's frown. "I mean, heck. You don't let me do nothing."

"I'll let you do some math," Julie said.

Caleb chuckled at Will's outraged expression. "You did rather walk into that one, son."

"What kinda math?" Will asked cautiously.

"You explain to him, Julie, while I go tell Miss Vincent we're here so she can leave," Caleb said.

"Okay." Julie felt a sense of warm contentment at Caleb's words. They made the three of them sound like a family. Sharing the responsibility so that things ran smoothly. But they weren't a family, she reminded herself as she watched Caleb walk into the house. She might be madly in love with him and inordinately fond of his son, but other than a few kisses she'd seen no signs that he felt anything other than friendship for her.

Julie bit back a sudden urge to burst into tears. She was sick and tired of being everyone's friend. She wanted to be someone's everything. She wanted to be the center of their existence. She wanted…her head examined, she thought dispiritedly. She simply wasn't the type to incite a grand passion in a man, and she ought to know it by now.

"What's the matter, Julie?"

Will slipped his small hand into hers.

"Don't look so sad. I'll do the math," he said.

Julie hastily pulled herself out of the morass of self-pity that was threatening to consume her.

"Did I look sad? I'm not," she lied. "How could I be? I just bought a new car, and I'm about to spend the afternoon with you and your father working on the tree house."

"Really?" Will's eyes began to gleam with eagerness. "Are we really going to start today?"

"We sure are. You and I are going to measure the boards to make sure they are long enough and…"

"And your father is going to saw them off where you two mark them," Caleb added as he rejoined them. "Then Julie and I will nail the boards into place up in the tree while you send up the nails."

"Saw?" Will ignored the rest. "With a saw like on television that goes whir and cuts right through the boards?"

"Don't even think it, Will." Julie barely suppressed a shudder at the images that leaped to mind. "Electric saws are very dangerous. I wouldn't use one."

"But that doesn't count. You're a girl," Will said.

"For your information, young man, I am not a girl. I am a woman."

She sure was. Caleb's eyes were instinctively drawn to the soft swell of her breasts. Julie Raffet was the epitome of womanhood. The woman of his dreams. Dreams that, until he'd meet Julie he hadn't even been aware that he'd had.

The problem was figuring out how to get her to see him as the man she wanted to spend the rest of her life with.

This wasn't the time to worry about it, Caleb told himself. Later, when he was alone, he could consider ways and means. Right now, he intended to savor every moment of his afternoon in her company.

"Mr. Tarrington." Miss Vincent emerged from the house. "I'm just off now, but there's a phone call for Ms. Raffet. I told them I wasn't sure you were still here," Miss Vincent told Julie. "So if you don't want to talk to them, you don't have to."

"Did they identify themselves?" Julie asked.

"Yes, a Miss Chatsfield. She said it was about some teaching position."

Julie smiled at Miss Vincent. "Thanks. I'll take it."

Julie hurried into the house, wondering what the hiring committee wanted this time. They'd already asked her enough questions to write a textbook.

To her surprise, the phone call wasn't about yet another question. It was about the job itself.

"What did they want this time?" Caleb asked.

Julie turned around to find Caleb and Will standing behind her.

"They just offered me the job," she said slowly, wondering why she wasn't more excited. This was the job she'd been trying to land ever since she'd first found out, two years ago, that a charter school would be opening. So why wasn't she dancing around the room in delight? She didn't know and that worried her.

"I thought you's gotta job at that school Dad says I gotta go to?" Will demanded belligerently.

"I do," Julie said. "This is another job."

"You don't need no nother job! I wants you to be where I is," Will said.

"Will, Julie is a teacher, and this is a big opportunity for her," Caleb tried to explain.

"There's kids at that school you gonna make me go to. Why can't she teach them?"

"This is Julie's decision," Caleb said flatly. "If she wants our advice, she'll ask for it. Now, let's get going on the tree house."

"Will ya let me saw one board? Just one? Please?" Will tried to bargain.

"No. You have to be older to operate an electric saw," Caleb said.

"How old?" Will demanded.

"A teenager." Caleb grabbed the age out of the air.

"Rats! I'll never get to be a teenager." He stomped off to the patio.

"I shudder to think what that kid's going to be like when he's had a few more years to perfect his arguments," Caleb said.

Julie chuckled at Caleb's worried expression. "Probably pretty much like you were."

"If you're finished trying to terrorize me, shall we follow the kid before he figures out something else to get into that I haven't expressly forbidden?

"And congratulations on the job offer," Caleb said. "You must be very pleased."

"Yes, I am," Julie said, because it was the answer he clearly expected. And she was pleased, she assured herself. But it was such a mild sense of pleasure. Not even close to the pleasure she got from simply looking at Caleb. And as for when she was actually kissing him...

"Would you two hurry up!" Will yelled from the patio. "We's never gonna get my tree house done."

"Coming," Julie called out to him. If only it were that easy to turn a dream into a reality, she thought. If only life came with blueprints for convincing the man you loved that you were essential to his happiness. If only, Julie thought grimly. It sounded like the story of her life.

Chapter Ten

"Night, son." Caleb leaned over and kissed Will's forehead. "Sleep tight, and don't let the bedbugs bite."

"What!" Will's sleepy eyes shot open with sudden interest. "Has we got bugs? Really?"

He lifted his bed covers and peered beneath them hopefully.

"Don't even suggest such a thing or Miss Vincent will have our heads."

"But you said—"

"Sorry, it's something my grandmother used to say when she'd tuck me into bed when I was about your age. It's just an old expression. It doesn't mean anything."

"Didn't you have a mother to tuck you in neither?" Will asked curiously.

"Yes, and she did a very good job of it, too," Caleb said.

"Where is she?"

Caleb felt a momentary surge of sadness at the thought that Will would never know either his grandmother or his great-grandmother. They had been such wonderful women. Perfect role models for a child. Much like Julie was.

"She died when I was in college," Caleb said.

"Oh." Will considered the information for a moment and then said, "But, Julie, she ain't dead."

"True, but I don't understand the connection."

"Well, my grandma and my great-grandma can't tuck me in, but Julie could. If'n she lived here with us."

Caleb studied his son's earnest features for a long moment.

"But the only way she could live here is if we were to marry her," Caleb said slowly, holding his breath for Will's answer. It would remove a huge obstacle if Will was in favor of his marrying Julie.

"You gotta marry her, Dad, 'cause I ain't old enough," Will said earnestly. "Then she can live here and tuck me in, and she can be my mom. Julie, she likes me. She likes me just the way I am. She don't think I's a nuisance."

"No, she doesn't. Neither do I, for that matter," Caleb said. "But I'm not sure that Julie would want to marry me."

"Has you asked her?" Will demanded.

"No," Caleb said.

"Then how do you know she might not like it? You gotta ask. Then we'll know."

But what if he asked her and she said no? A shudder rippled through Caleb, chilling his skin as his underlying fear popped to the surface of his thoughts. The fear that so far had stopped him from acting on his love for her. If she said no, he'd lose what he did have. He'd lose her companionship. He'd lose her laughter, and he'd lose the fantastic sensuality of her kisses. But if she said yes… He felt his breath catch in his throat at the magnitude of what he would gain.

"Dad!" The impatient sound of Will's voice penetrated Caleb's thoughts.

"It isn't that simple, Will," Caleb tried to explain.

"'Course not," Will scoffed. "First ya gotta tell her you love her like they do in the movies. Even I know that."

"You do, huh? Maybe you ought to be the one who does the proposing for me?

"No! I was joking," Caleb hastily backtracked when Will's small features brightened. "She's not likely to believe I love her if you tell her. She'll think it's just something you cooked up."

Will's face fell. "Probably. But we ain't got all day here, Dad. We gotta grab her before someone else does."

"I'll ask her," Caleb said, and the words came out like a vow. "But I'll do it when I think the time is right and not before."

"Okay." Will snuggled down under his covers. "I won't mind so much that Julie ain't at my new school if'n I get to see her every day at home."

Caleb turned out the light in Will's room and slowly walked back to the recreation room. The house was so quiet. So empty without Julie there. He could almost feel her presence lingering in the air from this afternoon. Could almost hear her laughter still echoing in the kitchen from when the three of them had made dinner.

Caleb poured himself a straight scotch and sank

down into an oversize leather chair to think. He knew what he wanted to do. He wanted to marry Julie. He wanted her to be living in his house with him. He wanted to share his days' events with her every evening. He wanted to spend his nights with her.

He took a deep swallow of the scotch as visions of making love to Julie flooded his mind. First things first. He squashed the images with an effort. First, he had to convince her to marry him. But how could he maximize his chance of success?

He chewed on his lower lip as he considered ways and means. Just coming out and asking her was too risky. She might turn him down. Even telling her that he loved her first was risky. She might not believe him. She might think that he was just saying it to get a mother for Will.

No, somehow, he had to figure out a way to show Julie how much he loved her. He took another sip of the scotch as he tried to figure it out.

Flowers? He considered and then immediately discarded the idea when he remembered Joe and the huge bouquet he'd brought to her. No, flowers were too easy to buy. And she already knew he had enough money to buy her anything she wanted, so buying something wasn't going to convince her of anything.

He frowned slightly as he remembered something she had once said about Prince Charming. Something about not being the type of woman to attract Prince Charming. She was, of course. In fact, as far as he was concerned, Julie Raffet was the embodiment of every feminine charm known to man.

His eyes narrowed in thought. Maybe he could use one of the fairy tales she'd mentioned to show her how much he loved her?

The more Caleb considered the idea the more he liked it. The only problem was that he wasn't sure which fairy tale he could use. He searched his memory, but other than a few references to impossibly beautiful heroines and equally impossible evil villains, he couldn't come up with any specifics. Fairy tales had not been a big part of his childhood. He just hoped he could successfully incorporate at least one of them into his adult life.

Tomorrow was Sunday. Julie wasn't coming to tutor Will, but she had mentioned that she intended to spend the day working on her yard and preparing for a graduate class she was to start next week. So he could count on her being at home where he could find her.

Right after church, he'd stop by the bookstore and pick up the biggest book on fairy tales they had, he decided. Then he'd read it and figure out which one he could use to convince Julie he loved her.

Excitement began to bubble through him. With any luck at all, by tomorrow night Julie would have agreed to marry him and, if he were really lucky, she'd agree to a quick wedding. He wouldn't feel secure again until they were safely married.

Caleb leaned back again in his chair and allowed the intoxicating thought of actually being married to Julie fill his mind.

"That's fantastic, Julie. Congratulations!" Darcie's voice sounded crystal clear over her cell phone from Vermont. "When do you start your new job?"

"I haven't resigned my old one yet," Julie said slowly.

"Why not? I thought this charter-school job was a big opportunity."

"It is, but…" Julie couldn't put her reluctance to commit herself into words without going into her love for Caleb. Accepting a job at the new school would cut her last remaining link with him. At least at the old school Will would be there, and she could see him every day. And, occasionally, Caleb. But she could hardly tell her levelheaded sister that. It sounded so pathetic. Like she were a lovelorn heroine in some badly written soap opera.

"There's something you aren't telling me," Darcie immediately picked up on the odd note in Julie's voice. "What?"

"You're imagining things," Julie said. "Tell me why you're still in Vermont. I thought you'd be home by now."

"I thought so too, but I've run into a hitch. The owner of the patent isn't too keen to sell."

"Try smiling at him. Mom always said your smile would convince the devil to join the Church again," Julie said, trying to keep her sister talking about her own problems. Darcie was like a bulldog. Once she got her teeth into something, she never let go.

It was bad enough that she had fallen in love with Caleb Tarrington, especially after Darcie had warned her of the hopelessness of doing it, but to have to admit it and then listen to her sister try to make her feel better was more than Julie could stand at the moment. She wanted to lick her wounds in private. That and enjoy what time she had left with Caleb without a lot of well-meaning advice about cutting her losses and not seeing him anymore.

"Baloney," Darcie muttered. "Let me tell you something, sister. Being beautiful isn't all that great."

Julie chuckled. "It sure beats not being beautiful."

"I'm serious," Darcie insisted. "I never know if a guy likes me or if he just likes the ego booster of escorting a beautiful woman."

"Maybe," Julie said slowly, taken aback at Darcie's words. "But the problem with just being attractive is that men tend not to see you at all."

"I don't want men in the plural. I just want one. But never mind my problems. Tell me why you haven't accepted the new job."

"Oh, I'm sorry, Darcie, but I have to run. Someone's at the door," she lied.

"All right," Darcie gave up. "I'll give you a call when I get back, and we can talk then."

"Okay." Julie hung up with relief. Thank God her sister was occupied with the troubles she was having with the patent. Otherwise she would never have given up so easily. Darcie had always taken her role as big sister very seriously, but this was the first time Julie could ever remember that it had grated on her.

Julie sank down on the sofa, letting her breath out on a long sigh. Falling in love with Caleb had changed everything. All her old relationships seemed to be shifting to make room for her new one. The problem was, the new relationship didn't exist anywhere except in her own mind. There wasn't the slightest hint that Caleb saw her as anything more than a friend. Even the fact that he'd kissed her didn't mean much in this day and age. Caleb wasn't some callow boy. He was a man, and a sophisticated one at that. What she saw as the fulfillment of every fantasy she'd ever had about kissing, he probably saw as nothing more than a pleasant interlude, signifying nothing. Although…

Julie remembered Darcie's words. She had certainly sounded serious about wishing she weren't quite so gorgeous. And when she thought about it, she could see that Darcie might have a point. Never knowing if a man liked you for yourself or simply liked the envy other men felt when they saw you with him would not make one feel very secure.

She might not know why Caleb had kissed her, but one thing she did know. He wasn't doing it because of her looks.

Restless and thoroughly out of sorts, Julie got to her feet and went into the bathroom to find some aspirin for the nagging headache behind her eyes. The day seemed endless without even the possibility of seeing Caleb. She glanced at the clock. Eleven-thirty. Almost twenty-one hours before she could see him again.

Caleb pitched the book he'd been reading onto the couch with a disgusted snort. He'd been reading fairy tales for more than an hour, and the only conclusion he'd come to was that they were peopled with massively dysfunctional individuals. There hadn't been a single character who'd even vaguely approached what he considered normal. Taking one of them for a role model would land him in jail, provided he didn't wind up in a psychiatric ward first.

"I coulda told you that book wasn't no good." Will looked up from his own book. "I had me a nanny once that used t'read fairy tales to me. They's really dumb."

"I'll say," Caleb agreed. Maybe liking fairy tales was a female thing.

Satisfied that his father agreed with him, Will returned to the *Star Trek* book he was reading.

Now what? Caleb wondered. How could he use one of those warped personalities as a role model? But maybe he didn't actually have to use a fairy-tale character? The glimmer of an idea stirred in his mind. Maybe the real appeal of fairy tales for women was the extravagant gestures the so-called heroes made. Like Prince Charming searching the kingdom for his lost love.

Maybe a gesture was all that it would take. But what kind of gesture could he make that would convince Julie that he loved her to the point of distraction and wanted to marry her and spend the rest of his life with her?

Lochinvar! He suddenly remembered a poem he'd been forced to read in high school. His eyes narrowed as he tried to remember how it had gone. It had had something to do with feuds, and the hero arriving at his beloved's wedding to another man, sweeping her up on his horse and riding off into the sunset with her.

That certainly qualified as a grand gesture, Caleb thought with satisfaction. No woman could possibly mistake Lochinvar's intentions.

So how could he adapt Lochinvar's gesture to his own situation? Horses were out. He hadn't been on a horse since Boy Scout camp. But the modern metaphor for a horse was a car. He certainly had one of those. He could sweep her up in his arms, carry her down to the car, pop her in and...

And what? The trouble with driving off into the sunset was that the sun also rose.

Forget tomorrow. Caleb firmly suppressed his practical nature. The day after wasn't important. The gesture was everything. He would sweep Julie up in his arms, put her in his car and drive her out to his grandfather's summer cottage on the lake. It was a short ride, but it was also miles from anywhere. There would be nothing and no one to distract her while he made his case. His grandfather had kept it purposely isolated as a retreat from the pressure of the real world.

He'd do it right away, he decided. This afternoon. Before he lost his nerve. He didn't know if his idea would work or not, but he didn't have another one. Grand gestures were rather hard to come by in this day and age.

He'd ask Miss Vincent to stay after lunch was served and keep an eye on Will.

"Is you going somewhere this afternoon?" Will asked after Miss Vincent had agreed to stay until six.

"I'm going to go see Julie and ask her to marry me," Caleb announced, and the very act of verbalizing his intentions made him feel as if he'd reached the point of no return. But in reality he'd reached that point the minute he'd laid eyes on Julie, he realized with the wisdom of hindsight. Everything else that had happened in the meantime had simply been to bring him to this point.

"Say, Dad, when Julie marries us, maybe we can go to her church. She said her church has a special service just fer us kids. Julie says they don't make 'em listen to a boring old man."

"Maybe," Caleb murmured while the delightful words "when Julie marries us" echoed in his ears. If only things were that easy. But easy or not, he was committed now. Committed to his grand gesture and committed to Julie. No matter what.

An hour later, Caleb had replayed the coming scene with Julie over and over in his mind. Dominating each scenario were graphic images of everything that could go wrong. A circumstance that did nothing for his self-confidence.

He'd forced himself to eat his lunch, given Will a hug, thanked the curious Miss Vincent for watching Will on a Sunday afternoon and climbed into his car, feeling a lot like the soldiers from another poem who had charged into the valley of death.

"Buck up, Tarrington," he muttered to himself as he drove to Julie's house. "What could go wrong?"

A shudder racked his body as several of the more lurid possibilities flooded his mind.

"Bad choice of clichés," he muttered to himself. "Focus on what you can control."

Nervously, Caleb checked his gas gauge. Running out of gas in the middle of his grand gesture would turn it into a farce. The gauge read a comfortable three-fourths full. He touched his back pocket and felt the reassuring bulge of his wallet. He had money.

The outside factors were all accounted for. Now it was up to him to pull off the main event. The thought brought him no comfort whatsoever. He was so far outside his regular area of expertise that he had no guidelines to rely on. If anyone would have told him a month ago that on this Sunday afternoon he would be about to kidnap a woman, he would have laughed himself sick.

But then, a month ago he wouldn't have believed that a woman could ever mean to him what Julie now meant to him. He wasn't even sure a month ago that

he believed in love between a man and a woman.
Lust, yes. He believed in that. But he'd had grave
doubts about the kind of emotion that transcended the
physical. The kind of emotion that made a man want
to protect a woman and put her needs and wants
above his own.

Caleb turned onto Julie's street and every thought
drained from his mind, leaving him feeling weak and
shaky. Somehow he had to step outside his normal,
rather conventional personality and pull this off. He
had to. Everything depended on it.

Caleb pulled up in front of Julie's house and cut
the engine. He took a deep steadying breath, counted
to ten, added a muddled prayer and then fatalistically
stepped out of the car.

This is it, Tarrington, he told himself as he started
up the walk. Don't blow it.

Julie reached the end of the editorial she was reading and then grimaced when she realized that she
couldn't remember a single point the writer had made.
She dropped the paper and sighed. This was awful,
she couldn't even focus on something as elemental as
the Sunday paper. Thoughts of Caleb kept interfering.

Think about something constructive, she ordered
herself. Think about what you're going to do about
that job offer. Think about what you are going to do
to counter your obsession with Caleb Tarrington.

The thought of Caleb immediately brought in its
wake a host of images that had nothing to do with
practicality. Images of Caleb smiling at her. Of the
way he sat at his desk in the office reading, his dear
face taut with concentration. Images of him kissing
her, his features sharpened with sensual need. Need

that she had created. Need that she wanted to satisfy. Images...

"Your door is open again." Caleb's deep voice poured through her mind, adding color to her thoughts. He sounded so...

Real! She glanced up to see him standing in front of her open door.

"Caleb!" She jumped to her feet. "What are you doing here?" A sharp stab of fear shafted through her. "Is something wrong with Will?"

"No," Caleb said.

She breathed a sigh of relief. "Come in."

She pushed open the screen door.

To her surprise, instead of entering, he remained on the porch staring at her.

"Caleb?" Julie stepped out onto the porch, drawn by the intensity of his expression. He looked... She studied his lean features, trying to label this unexpected mood of his.

Determined, she finally decided. Very determined, but about what she had no idea.

"Caleb," she repeated, and then let out a startled squeak when without any warning he suddenly swept her up in his arms. Julie grabbed his neck to steady herself and then lost all interest in explanations when the scent of his cologne touched her senses. She closed her eyes the better to savor the smell and immediately became aware of the frantic thudding of his heart. Since she already knew that he was in great physical shape from the ease with which he climbed trees, the only other explanation for his rapid heartbeat she could think of had to be that he found holding her in his arms exciting. The thought sent a shiver of desire through her.

She didn't know what he was doing or why he was doing it. Nor had she any intention of asking. An explanation would reduce this to the commonplace. She preferred to live with the possibilities of what it might mean as long as she could.

She tightened her grip around his neck as he strode down the porch steps to his car.

"Hey! What's going on over there?" the voice of her elderly next-door neighbor intruded, and for the first time in her life Julie wished she had neighbors who minded their own business.

Caleb came to a stop beside the passenger side of his car and, balancing Julie's slight body against his own with one arm, reached down and awkwardly fumbled with the door handle.

Damn! he thought in exasperation. He should have settled for the horse. There weren't any handles on horses to contend with.

"If'n you don't tell me this instant what you're doing with Julie, I'm going to call the cops," Gus threatened. "And I got your license-plate number, too."

Frustrated by a complication he hadn't even considered, Caleb glared at Gus. "What the hell do you think I'm doing! I'm abducting her."

Sounds good to me, Julie thought, snuggling closer to him to offer encouragement. A good teacher always encouraged creativity.

Gus eyed Julie, who simply grinned at him. Finally Gus chuckled, muttered something about the impetuosity of modern youth and slowly went back into his house.

Caleb breathed a sigh of relief at having surmounted one unexpected obstacle. And then a second, when he finally managed to get the passenger door open. He gently placed Julie on the seat and closed it behind her.

Then he sprinted around to the driver's side to get in before she had a chance to change her mind and escape. Not that she'd voiced any objections yet. He took heart from that fact.

Julie waited until he had started the car and pulled into the street before she asked, "Why are you abducting me?"

"Because I thought...I mean..."

Julie felt a sharp stab of excitement at his disjoined words. Caleb was not an inarticulate man. If this were nothing more than a joke he'd thought up with Will, he wouldn't sound this distracted. This sounded as if he was emotionally involved in this, whatever *this* was.

"Yes?" she pushed.

"It's a gesture," he blurted out. "A grand gesture."

Julie considered his words. They didn't make any sense.

"I don't understand," she finally said.

"Join the club," he muttered. "It's really very simple. Lochinvar was the only one I could use as a pattern, and a horse was out."

At her blank expression, he plowed on.

"I spent this morning reading fairy tales and, let me tell you, those stories are filled with dysfunctional people."

"They're just morality plays from another time," Julie disposed of fairy tales.

"Whatever. I wanted to show you how I felt. Not tell you. Words are cheap."

"I don't know about cheap, but yours are certainly incomprehensible," Julie said.

"I..." Caleb took a deep breath, gathered his courage and said, "I wanted to show you how much I love you. Not just tell you. And since you said you could never be a heroine in a fairy tale, I wanted to show you that, as far as I was concerned, you already were. I just couldn't find an appropriate fairy tale that I could adapt. So I went with a poem I remembered about a guy named Lochinvar who abducted the woman he loved and rode off into the sunset with her."

Julie simply stared at Caleb's features as a joy so intense that it made her dizzy filled her. Caleb loved her. He actually saw her as the heroine of his own personal fairy tale!

She swallowed, and her lower lip trembled beneath the force of her emotions. There was no possibility of mistaking what he felt. It was there in his face for the whole world to read. And there in his actions to try to prove it to her.

Darcie had been right once again. It didn't matter how most men saw her. All that mattered was how one man saw her. As long as it was the right one.

Caleb shot a quick glance at her, and his heart sank as he saw her quivering lower lip and the tears that filled her eyes.

"Don't cry," he said. "I didn't mean to upset you."

"Upset! I am so happy I think I could fly."

"Happy?" Caleb asked cautiously, almost afraid to believe her.

"That really doesn't begin to describe what I feel," Julie said. "I want to grab you and kiss you and stick my head out the window and tell the whole world that we love each other and..."

"You love me?" Caleb latched onto the most important part.

"Madly, extravagantly, wholeheartedly."

"Damn!" Caleb said in frustration. "Lochinvar was right to use a horse. How can I kiss you while I'm driving a car?"

"You can't," Julie conceded. "So let's go to your house and tell Will."

"Your house, too," Caleb said with satisfaction. "And Will'll be ecstatic. He has all kinds of plans for when 'we' marry Julie."

Julie laughed, and her happiness lent an added sparkle to the sound. "Will is the most delightful child. If we're really lucky, maybe we'll have a couple more just like him."

Caleb felt her words slam into him, and it was all he could do to concentrate on getting them safely home. Grimly, he forced himself to think of something other than the intoxicating thought of making babies with Julie.

"I want you to understand that I have no intention of interfering with your career, Julie. I know how much it means to you, and I also know how much good you do for the kids."

"I appreciate that." Julie sighed, feeling the last niggling doubt she'd had dissolve beneath his obvious sincerity. "And I do intend to keep teaching, but not at the new charter school."

"No?" Caleb frowned uncertainly. "Why not? I thought you really wanted that job."

"I did when I was single. Getting everything set up at that job would have involved giving up evenings and weekends for at least a year. Now that I'm going to have a family of my own, I'd much rather spend my free time with you and Will. I'll just stay with my regular job at Whittier.''

Family. Caleb tasted the word and found it incredibly sweet.

''Yes,'' he said with intense satisfaction as he headed for home. ''We are a family. Now and forever.''

''Forever,'' Julie repeated, and the words echoed around the car like a vow.

*   *   *   *   *

Warning: Fairy tales do come true!

brings you an irresistible new series

by **Lilian Darcy**

The three Brown sisters don't believe in
happily-ever-afters—until each one is rescued
by her own gallant knight!

September 2001
Cinderella After Midnight—SR #1542

November 2001
Saving Cinderella—SR #1555

January 2002—
Finding Her Prince—SR #1567

Available at your favorite retail outlet.

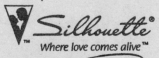
Where love comes alive™

Visit Silhouette at www.eHarlequin.com   SRCIN

Coming in January 2002,
from Silhouette Books
and award-winning, bestselling author

ANNETTE
BROADRICK

Secret Agent Grooms

Three heartbreaking men who'll risk their lives—
but not their hearts!

In ADAM'S STORY, a man in search of his enemy
finds love where he least expected it....

In THE GEMINI MAN, an undercover agent assigned
to protect a damsel in distress finds himself bringing
his work home with him!

In ZEKE, a woman who thinks Zeke has been
assigned to protect her learns he's really after
her uncle. But he's not quite through
with her yet, either....

SECRET AGENT GROOMS:
They're always around when you need them!

Available at your favorite retail outlet.

Silhouette®
Where love comes alive™

Visit Silhouette at www.eHarlequin.com   BR3SAG

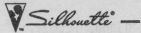

Silhouette®
where love comes alive—online...

eHARLEQUIN.com

your romantic
books

♥ **Shop online!** Visit Shop eHarlequin and discover a wide selection of new releases and classic favorites at great discounted prices.

♥ **Read** our daily and weekly Internet exclusive serials, and participate in our interactive novel in the reading room.

♥ **Ever dreamed of being a writer?** Enter your chapter for a chance to become a featured author in our Writing Round Robin novel.

your romantic
life

♥ **Check out** our feature articles on dating, flirting and other important romance topics and get your daily love dose with tips on how to keep the romance alive every day.

♥ **Learn** what the stars have in store for you with our daily Passionscopes and weekly Erotiscopes.

♥ **Get** the latest scoop on your favorite royals in Royal Romance.

your
community

♥ **Have a Heart-to-Heart** with other members about the latest books and meet your favorite authors.

♥ **Discuss** your romantic dilemma in the Tales from the Heart message board.

All this and more available at
www.eHarlequin.com

SINTA1R2

SOME MEN ARE BORN TO BE ROYALTY.
OTHERS ARE MADE...

CROWNED HEARTS

A royal anthology featuring,
NIGHT OF LOVE, a classic novel from
international bestselling author

DIANA PALMER

Plus a brand-new story in the MacAllister family series by

JOAN ELLIOT PICKART

and a brand-new story by

LINDA TURNER,

which features the royal family of the upcoming
ROMANCING THE CROWN series!

Available December 2001 at your favorite retail outlet.

Where love comes alive™

Visit Silhouette at www.eHarlequin.com   PSCH

New from

a sperm bank mix-up sets a
powerful executive in search
of the woman who's...

Don't miss any of these titles from
this exciting new miniseries:

WHEN THE LIGHTS WENT OUT...,
October 2001 by Judy Christenberry

A PREGNANT PROPOSAL,
November 2001 by Elizabeth Harbison

THE MAKEOVER TAKEOVER,
December 2001 by Sandra Paul

LAST CHANCE FOR BABY,
January 2002 by Julianna Morris

SHE'S HAVING MY BABY!,
February 2002 by Raye Morgan

Available at your favorite retail outlet.

Where love comes alive™

Visit Silhouette at www.eHarlequin.com

SRHBB

sensual to him. Even worse, he was clearly worried that she might read something into his action. The thought stiffened her pride as nothing else could have.

"Don't worry about it." She forced a breezy note into her voice. "I have been held in a man's arms before. Now, why don't you go back to work while I clean up this mess." She attempted to get rid of him while she regained her composure.

A flash of intense emotion that he had no trouble labeling as plain old jealousy ripped through him. He didn't want other men holding Julie.

What was happening to him? Caleb wondered in confusion. He was normally an even-tempered man. So why did his emotions feel as if they were on a runaway roller coaster every time he was around Julie Raffet? Maybe his reaction was caused by the fact that he was already off balance emotionally from finding out he had a son. Maybe it was nothing more than that. He clung to the face-saving explanation, trying hard to believe it.

"If you should want me, I'll be in my office," Caleb said, hoping his words didn't sound like the retreat they were.

With a nod at Julie, he hurriedly left.

Julie sagged up against the door frame of the closet, and her breath escaped in a ragged sigh of relief. She'd done it. She'd convinced Caleb that being in his arms hadn't affected her one bit. So now what? She tried to come up with a plan of action. Where did she go from here?

Julie closed her eyes to think and immediately saw a tantalizing image of Caleb painted on the back of her eyelids. He was leaning toward her, his features taut with desire.